AN INNOCENT IN RUSSIA

She lifted her face and he looked down at her for a long moment before his lips found hers.

As he kissed her Zelina knew that his was what she had been waiting and longing for ever since they had been together on the *Ischora*.

Lord Charnock's lips were gentle and tender, and as he felt her mouth quiver beneath his he knew it was the first time she had been kissed, and how innocent and inexperienced she was.

Bantam Books by Barbara Cartland
Ask your bookseller for the books you have missed

A NEW SERVICE FOR
BARBARA CARTLAND READERS

Now you can have the latest Barbara Cartland romances delivered to your home automatically each month. For further information on this new reader service, contact the Direct Response Department, Bantam Books, 666 Fifth Avenue, New York, N. Y. 10103. Phone (212) 765-6500.

An Innocent
in
Russia

Barbara Cartland

BANTAM BOOKS

TORONTO · NEW YORK · LONDON · SYDNEY

AN INNOCENT IN RUSSIA
A Bantam Book/November 1981

ISBN 0-553-20126-3

Published simultaneously in the United States and Canada

Bantam Books are published by Bantam Books, Inc. Its trade-
mark, consisting of the words "Bantam Books" and the por-
trayal of a rooster, is Registered in U.S. Patent and Trademark
Office and in other countries. Marca Registrada. Bantam
Books, Inc., 666 Fifth Avenue, New York, New York 10103.

PRINTED IN THE UNITED STATES OF AMERICA

0 9 8 7 6 5 4 3 2 1

Author's Note

Although the hero and heroine of this novel are fictitious, most of the other characters are real and the background is factual.

I am deeply grateful for details from *The Russian Journal of Lady Londonderry*, written about the same journey she and her husband, the "proud Marquis," took to Russia in 1836, and to that entrancing history *The Romanovs* by Virginia Cowles.

Tsar Nicholas I was undoubtedly the most alarming Sovereign in Europe. His ice-cold eyes struck such terror into the hearts of his courtiers that one of them, after his death, confessed that he kept the Emperor's portrait turned to the wall.

"I had such a fear of the original," he said, "that even a copy with those terrible eyes frightens and embarrasses me."

The Secret Police in the "Third Section" terrorised the whole country, especially the intellectuals. No-one was safe from them, no-one knew where they would strike next.

Chapter One
1836

"Her Ladyship wants you, Miss Zelina!"

Zelina looked up from her book and gave a little sigh.

It was always the same—when she was reading something interesting, she was requested to do something else, and she was quite certain that whatever her aunt wanted, it would not be anything pleasant.

Ever since she had come to the big house in Grosvenor Square she had felt she was an encumbrance and not wanted.

It had been hard enough to lose her father the previous year and be left alone in their home in Gloucestershire, with only her old Governess who was growing deaf and could do little but sit in front of the fire with her knitting.

But at least Zelina had been free to ride every day in the Park, to walk in the woods, and to read.

That was what she enjoyed more than anything else, and the only consolation she had after her father's death was his huge Library of books.

Now when her mourning was over and she was eighteen, her aunt had sent for her to come to London, and as soon as she arrived she was aware that it was not because Aunt Kathleen intended to introduce her to the Social World.

Major Tiverton had always said that his younger

sister was a frivolous, tiresome woman, despite the fact that she was very beautiful.

"She was ambitious when she was in the cradle!" he would say to Zelina. "If it had been possible, she would have set her sights on marrying a King. As it was, she had to be content with that crashing bore Rothbury, and I expect she leads him a pretty dance!"

Zelina had not been particularly interested in her aunt, whom she had not seen since she was a child.

But when her father died she realised that as her Aunt Kathleen was her nearest relative, she was now in the position of being her Guardian.

Letters had been passed to and from London, not to her but to her father's Solicitors, who were handling the small amount of money left by Major Tiverton.

Of course, there were also the house and the Estate. Zelina had cried when she was told it would be the sensible thing to sell it so that she might have whatever it fetched as what the Solicitor called a "nest-egg" against the future.

"Not, I'm sure, that you'll need one, Miss Tiverton," he had added with a smile. "But even when she marries, it is useful for a woman to have a small dowry of her own."

Zelina had been aware that in his own way he was paying her a compliment, and she would have been very foolish if she had not known that most men looked at her, looked again, and a glint came into their eyes.

She thought humbly that she would never be as beautiful as her mother, but at least she was qretty and her father had often confirmed this.

"If there is one thing I cannot stand," he had said, "it is a plain woman! I am fortunate to have both a beautiful wife and a daughter who is a reflection of her."

When her mother died, Zelina had found it very difficult to console him, and he buried himself in his books just as she tried to do when she lost him.

As she journeyed to London, thinking how little she knew about the world that existed outside Gloucestershire, she found herself hoping that there would be a Library in her aunt's house.

There was, and it contained a lot of the latest and most up-to-date novels, but Zelina found that she had little time to read.

"Good Heavens, child! You look like a scarecrow!" her aunt had exclaimed as soon as she saw her. "Where can you have bought a gown like the one you are wearing?"

"I . . . I made it, Aunt Kathleen."

"That is what it looks like! I cannot allow any of my friends to see you until you are properly dressed."

Zelina was very conscious that she looked extremely dowdy beside her aunt. Never had she imagined that anybody could look so spectacularly gowned from first thing in the morning to last thing at night.

Zelina loved everything that was beautiful, but there had never been enough money for both horses and gowns, and horses had come first.

When she first arrived in Grosvenor Square it had been exciting to go with Aunt Kathleen to the shops in Bond Street, where she was fitted out with so many different gowns that she wondered if she would ever have a chance of wearing them all.

She soon learnt that a fashionable lady changed her clothes three or four times a day, and there were therefore complete *toilettes* for the morning, for luncheon, and for tea-time, and of course very alluring gowns for the evening.

But she found that she needed not only gowns but pelisses, shawls, bonnets, shoes, sunshades, and so many other things that she lost count.

She was aware that they would fill to overflowing the small wardrobe in her bedroom, and she would certainly need several more chests-of-drawers to accommodate the more intimate garments that her aunt had ordered by the dozen.

Choosing and ordering her clothes took nearly a week, the fittings longer.

During this time she was not allowed to appear anywhere where she could be seen by Aunt Kathleen's friends, and she dined downstairs only when the Earl and Countess of Rothbury were alone, which was very rare.

When she met the Earl, who was getting on in years and was extremely stout, Zelina found that her father had been right in saying he was a bore.

He never listened to anything anybody else had to say, but would talk deliberately and pompously on any subject which occurred to him, regardless of whether or not it interested those who were listening.

Zelina soon realised that her aunt paid no attention to anything her husband said, and it was very obvious that she lived her own life in her own circle of friends, which included some extremely attractive and attentive gentlemen.

One in particular was continually calling at the house in Grosvenor Square when the Earl was either at the House of Lords or at his Club.

Looking back afterwards, Zelina realised that her fate had been sealed when he was shown into the Drawing-Room unexpectedly and she met him for the first time.

"Harry!" the Countess had exclaimed when he was announced. "I was not expecting you."

"I know," Harry replied, "but I saw George puffing along Parliament Square and knew the coast was clear!"

Then he realised that Zelina was in the room and glanced at her curiously.

With an effort the Countess said:

"This is my niece Zelina Tiverton, who is staying with us."

Zelina curtseyed and her aunt added sharply:

"You have a lot of things to do in your own room, Zelina. I shall be busy for the next hour or so."

"Yes, of course, Aunt Kathleen," Zelina replied.

She walked across the room, conscious that Harry— she had not been told his full name—was watching her.

Then as she was shutting the door she heard him exclaim:

"That girl is a raving beauty! Why have I not seen her before?"

For two or three days there was an undoubted coolness in Aunt Kathleen's attitude, and she appeared to be uninterested when Zelina told her that most of her gowns and various accessories had arrived.

Because she had barely spoken to anybody except the servants since she had arrived in London, she was hoping that perhaps now her aunt would take her to one of the parties or Balls she attended every night, or even allow her to accompany her in her carriage when she went driving in Hyde Park.

Instead, there had been an ominous silence, and now as Zelina rose hastily to her feet she wondered why Aunt Kathleen wanted her.

It was rather early in the day for her to be sent for.

Because the Countess was out every evening, she seldom awoke before eleven o'clock, and only after she had breakfasted and opened her letters was Zelina allowed into her bedroom.

Now as she walked from her bedroom towards her aunt's, Zelina looked over the bannisters at the top of the stairs and saw that the grandfather clock showed that it was only half-after-ten.

The Countess's bedroom, which faced the front of the Square, was very large and impressive, with Chinese wallpaper and a huge bed draped with muslin and silk.

This was, Zelina knew, a copy of a fashion popular

in France, and the green of the bedspread was a reflection of the green in her aunt's eyes.

They could be warm and seductive or cold and very disapproving. As she neared the bed, she thought with a sinking of her heart that the latter was their expression at this moment.

There were a lot of letters lying in front of her aunt on the bedspread. She was holding one in her hand and looked at it for a long moment before she said:

"I have something to tell you, Zelina."

"Good-morning, Aunt Kathleen! I hope you slept well!" Zelina said, feeling apprehensive because her aunt had not greeted her in any way.

"What I have to tell you," the Countess went on as if Zelina had not spoken, "is that I have decided your immediate future, and I think you are an extremely fortunate young woman."

"Decided . . . my future, Aunt Kathleen?"

"That is what I said, and there is no need to repeat my words!" the Countess snapped. "You are going to Russia."

For a moment Zelina thought she could not have heard her correctly. Then, because she was so astonished, she could only stammer:

"D-did you say to . . . Russia?"

"Yes, Russia! As I have said, you are most fortunate, and it will be an experience which would make most young women feel overjoyed at the thought."

"B-but . . . why Russia, Aunt Kathleen? And what shall I . . . do there?"

"That is what I am going to tell you," the Countess said as if Zelina was being extremely half-witted. "After all, your Godmother from whom you received your name was Russian."

"But she is dead . . . and I cannot even . . . remember her."

"That is immaterial, but it should in a way give

you a link with Russia and make you appreciate the country."

"I am not . . . going alone?"

"Well, I am certainly not coming with you, if that is what you are supposing!" the Countess replied. "Let me make it quite clear, Zelina, I have no wish to chaperone you for the rest of the London Season and lug a young girl about with me. You certainly would not fit in with my circle of friends or the life I lead as your uncle's wife."

Zelina was intelligent enough to know that what her aunt was saying was that she had no desire to have with her another woman who might, although it seemed unlikely, prove a rival in some way.

Zelina was quite aware that she would be very much out-of-place among the witty, sophisticated friends with whom her aunt amused herself.

At the same time, it had never occurred to her, now that she had come to London and been given such a large wardrobe of attractive clothes, that she would at once be sent away.

The Countess was still carefully reading the letter she had in her hand. Then she said:

"I was of course thinking of you when I mentioned to the wife of the Russian Ambassador that you had a Russian Godmother and it was a pity she was not alive so that you could go and stay with her."

"She might not have . . . wanted me."

"I am quite certain she would have been delighted to have her Godchild with her," the Countess contradicted, "and that was what I told the Ambassadress. She agrees with me that it is very sad that you should miss the opportunity of visiting Russia, and she has therefore arranged it."

"Arranged . . . what?" Zelina asked in a frightened voice.

"That you should go out to Russia and stay with the

Prince and Princess Volkonsky, who will welcome you
as a—member of their household."

There was just a slight hesitation before the word
"member," and Zelina asked:

"What would be my position in the house, Aunt
Kathleen? Am I a guest, or am I being . . . employed in
some . . . way?"

She knew by the way the Countess looked at her
that she was embarrassed.

"You cannot expect to stay for any length of time in
any household unless you can contribute something
towards the expense they incur on your behalf."

Zelina drew in her breath.

"What am I . . . expected to . . . do, Aunt Kathleen?"

"The Princess has children of various ages . . ." the
Countess began.

"What you are saying," Zelina interrupted, "is that
I am to be their Governess."

The Countess put down the letter.

"Now, Zelina, I do not like that attitude or the way
you are speaking to me. I am trying to do what is best
for you, and you will surely appreciate that if you go to
Russia, it will give you a knowledge of the world which
has been sadly lacking in your education up until now."

"Papa considered I was very much more . . . knowl-
edgeable than . . . most girls of my . . . age."

"Your father's opinion was one thing, mine is another," the Countess replied. "I have watched you
closely since you have been here, and I consider you
very ignorant in all the things that matter where a
young woman is concerned."

"But you still . . . consider me capable of . . . teaching
children!"

"I have not said you are to teach anybody!" the
Countess snapped. "But because you are so ignorant,
you do not seem to be aware that the great aristocratic

families in Russia employ a number of European attendants for their families."

She paused, then continued slowly:

"The Ambassadress tells me that the Emperor's
children have a Scottish Nurse who has been with them
for nineteen years, besides which they have numerous
Governesses and teachers of many different nationali-
ties. Moreover, English and French are the languages
usually spoken in all the Royal Palaces."

"So I am to . . . teach English!" Zelina persisted.

"You will *speak* English," her aunt contradicted.
"You are English, and the Ambassadress is certain that
you will find Russia extremely congenial."

"How . . . long am I to . . . stay there?"

The words seemed to be dragged from Zelina's
lips.

She felt growing inside her the fear that she was
being taken away from everything that was familiar and
she would never be able to return.

The Countess shrugged her shoulders.

"Why should there be a time-limit on your visit?"

There was a little pause, then Zelina said:

"I am sorry, Aunt Kathleen . . . but, although as you
say it is an opportunity to see the world . . . I would
rather . . . stay in England. I am sure, if you find me a
nuisance . . . that as I have a little money of my own . . . I
could live with one of our cousins until I can think of
something . . . better I could . . . do."

"And what do you think that might be?" the Countess asked.

Zelina put up her chin.

"If I have to work, Aunt Kathleen, I would rather
work in England."

"And have people say I am not looking after you
properly?" the Countess asked angrily. "You seem to
have forgotten, Zelina, that now that your father is

dead, I am your Guardian, and as I have decided you are going to Russia, that is where you will go!"

Zelina was about to say defiantly that she would refuse, but then she remembered that until she married she was legally under the jurisdiction of her Guardian. In that capacity, her Aunt Kathleen could really do as she liked with her.

As if the Countess knew without words that Zelina had capitulated, she said:

"Now stop being a bore. I have certainly done my best by providing you with what is almost a trousseau of expensive clothes, and you will thank me by not making scenes but by going to Russia as you are told."

"When you bought me my clothes, for which I thanked you very . . . profusely, had you . . . this in . . . mind?"

Her aunt did not have to answer, for Zelina knew by the expression on her face that this was the truth.

After a moment's silence she said:

"When am I . . . expected to . . . leave?"

"Your travelling arrangements will be made by the Russian Embassy. I believe you will go in a British ship to Stockholm, then you will change to a Russian vessel which will take you to St. Petersburg."

Zelina did not answer, and after a moment the Countess said:

"Oh, for Heaven's sake, stop being sulky! You should thank me for what I have done for you, and certainly you must have some sense of adventure! Who knows? It may turn out to be the chance of a lifetime."

Zelina did not reply.

She merely curtseyed and went from the room. Only when she reached the sanctuary of her own bedroom did she sit down as if her legs would no longer carry her and put her hands up to her face.

It was not that she was not adventurous. She and

her father had often talked of how, if they could afford it, they would explore France, visit the Greek Islands, and perhaps, if it was possible, see a little of Africa.

But to go to Russia alone, to be cut off from everything that had been part of her life up to now, made Zelina, although she was ashamed of it, feel afraid.

She had never been particularly interested in Russia, although her mother had been very fond of her God-mother.

Whenever people met Zelina they always exclaimed at the strangeness of her name, and she often wished she had been christened differently.

Perhaps, she thought now, it had been a perception of what might happen in the future which had made her feel that Russia was a place that she had no wish to know about, and what she did know was not very reassuring.

She had read about Catherine the Great and her long succession of lovers, and the incredible cruelties of her son Tsar Paul.

She had no wish to learn any more about such people who apparently, while living in the height of luxury and fantastic extravagance, allowed the ordinary people of the country to suffer incredible privations.

"Russia!"

She felt a little shiver run through her at the thought that she must go away and be so far from the England she loved, which had filled her whole life until now.

She and her father had had so many friends where they lived, not only amongst the County families who had shown them many kindnesses, but also amongst the ordinary people in the village.

There had been workmen on their Estate, the old people in the Alms Houses whom her mother had visited regularly, and the pensioners who had known her father since he was a little boy and his father before him.

It had been hard to leave them when she came to London. At the same time, she had hoped to make new friends, girls of her own age who would perhaps share some of her interests.

And of course men whom she would talk to as she had talked to her father, and with whom, if they had been in the Army and were keen on horse-flesh, shooting, or hunting, she had common interests.

"But Russia!"

The words seemed to vibrate round her and grow louder and louder until she felt as if she were encountering the icy winds of Siberia which were terrifying her with their violence.

She took her hands from her face and rose to her feet.

"I will not go!" she said aloud. "I will run away!"

Then she knew that her aunt was determined to be rid of her and it would be extremely ignominious to be brought back if her escape should fail.

The Countess was not as empty-headed as her father had thought, and Zelina, having lived with her for nearly three weeks, was aware that she always got her own way.

The Earl might be of importance in the House of Lords, but in his house in Grosvenor Square he did what his wife wished.

It might be because he had no desire for a scene, but he was also, Zelina thought, genuinely proud of his wife's beauty and her place as one of the indisputable leaders of London Society.

'To him she is like a decoration he can pin on his coat to know that other people are envying him the possession of it,' Zelina thought shrewdly.

She was therefore quite certain that if she appealed

to the Earl for help he would merely tell her to obey her aunt, and for the moment she could think of nobody else to approach.

The only comfort was that in the Bank she had what seemed to her a quite considerable sum of money from the sale of her father's house and furniture.

"At least I shall be able to come home if I want to," she told herself.

She decided to make quite certain that she had enough money with her to pay for her return fare.

* * *

Having got her own way, as was inevitable, the Countess was quite pleasant for the next few days, but still she made no effort to take Zelina anywhere or to invite her to dine downstairs when there was a dinner-party.

Then she took her to tea alone with the Russian Ambassadress, which meant, Zelina knew, that she was being more or less interviewed for the position that she was to occupy in the Princess's house.

The Ambassadress had shrewd eyes and a sharp mind, which told Zelina that she missed nothing.

She gossipped with the Countess, but it was obvious that she was "looking over" her niece and calculating what impression she would make in St. Petersburg.

When it was time to leave, she said to Zelina:

"Enjoy yourself. The Russian character is difficult to understand, but its very complexity makes its people some of the most interesting as well as the most unpredictable in the world!"

Zelina smiled. It was not what she had expected to hear. Then as the Countess moved towards the door, the Ambassadress added:

"Keep a diary. You will find it interesting to look back and read it to your grandchildren when you have some."

What she said seemed to Zelina to lighten a little her fear of the future.

Nevertheless, when the day of departure arrived she felt as if she were being sent into exile and would never see England again.

The Countess with great condescension escorted her to Tilbury to take her on board the English ship which was to carry her as far as Stockholm.

Zelina was well aware that she would not have done this if the Russian Ambassador had not said he was sending an official from the Embassy to see to all the travelling arrangements.

"This is really very inconvenient for me," the Countess complained to Zelina.

"I am sorry, Aunt Kathleen, but you will not be seeing me for a very long time."

She thought that at this remark there was an expression of pleasure on the Countess's face, but she merely said:

"The Ambassador has given instructions to somebody on the ship to see you aboard the Russian vessel to which you will transfer at Stockholm."

Because the Countess disliked travelling, they spoke very little until they reached Tilbury, where Zelina saw she was to travel by steam-ship.

In the last few years steam-ships had been used for crossing the North Sea, the Straits of Dover, and the Irish Sea, after previously being used only as passenger-carriers along the coast to holiday resorts.

The ship which was to carry Zelina to Stockholm had auxiliary sails which would accelerate its speed and side paddle-wheels.

When they boarded the ship, the Countess asked to see the Passenger List, and read it with the expression of one who does not expect to find any acquaintance amongst a collection of nonentities.

Then she gave a little cry like that of someone who

has found treasure where she least expected it, and without saying anything to Zelina, who merely followed her, she went to the Purser's office.

"Has Lord Charnock come aboard yet?" she enquired.

"No, M'Lady," the Purser replied, "but His Lordship will doubtless arrive at any moment."

The Countess stood with a faint smile on her face as she waited, watching the gangway.

Sure enough, two or three minutes later a tall, distinguished-looking man wearing a travelling-cape lined with fur, and followed by an attendant carrying several important-looking despatch-cases bearing the Royal coat-of-arms, came aboard.

The Countess moved towards him with the smile on her lips which she reserved for those with whom she wished to ingratiate herself.

"My Lord!" she exclaimed. "This is an unexpected pleasure!"

Watching, Zelina had the impression that for Lord Charnock it was something very different.

She thought he was one of the most handsome men she had ever seen, but also one of the most aloof—or perhaps the right word was "inhuman."

There was something cold and distant about him, almost, she thought, as if there were no blood running in his veins and he was made of stone rather than flesh.

She did not know why she had this impression, but she was used to summing people up as soon as she saw them, and her father would often laugh at what he called the "pen-and-ink" sketches she would give of somebody to whom she had just been introduced or had met casually in the hunting-field.

'Lord Charnock,' she thought to herself now, 'is an intimidating man who is very sure of his own consequence.'

"Are you travelling on this ship?" she heard him ask her aunt drily.

"No, indeed," the Countess replied, "I am merely seeing off my niece, who is on her way to St. Petersburg. As she is travelling alone, it would be extremely kind of Your Lordship if you would keep an eye on her."

Zelina knew by the expression on Lord Charnock's face that this was something he had no wish to do, and he had no intention of accepting such a responsibility.

"I am afraid . . ." he began.

But in the Countess he had met his match.

"That is very kind of you," she said, "and I am extremely grateful."

He started to say something, but before he could do so she turned to Zelina.

"And now I must leave you, dear child. Take care of yourself. Enjoy your visit, and I am sure you will find it very rewarding."

Before Zelina could reply, her aunt had kissed her on the cheek, and then with a rustle of silk, the feathers on her bonnet blowing in the wind, she was moving quickly down the gangplank.

By the time she had reached the Quay, Zelina realised that Lord Charnock had disappeared and she thought with a little smile that she did not blame him.

It was typical of her aunt, she thought, to try to involve him because he was the only important person she knew on the Passenger List.

She did not know that her aunt was in fact paying off an old score against a man she disliked.

In his cabin, which was one of the most comfortable on the ship, Lord Charnock decided that the Countess of Rothbury's niece could, as far as he was concerned, look after herself.

He was well aware that Kathleen Rothbury had two years ago set out to capture his attention and, if possible, his heart, because it would have been a feather in her cap.

As the greatest beauty in Society she considered it an insult if any man whom she met at all frequently was not enslaved by her looks and ready to cast himself at her feet.

It had been an experience that had startled her when Lord Charnock had made it unmistakably clear that he did not find her attractive and, what was more, disliked her.

To the Countess this was completely incomprehensible, and although she had searched for an explanation, she could not find one.

What she did not know was that Lord Charnock considered that she had behaved extremely cruelly to a young man in the Foreign Office whom she had taken up for several months and then dropped because somebody more interesting occupied her attention.

The man in question was little more than a boy, and, believing his heart to be broken, he had asked to be sent overseas, although in Lord Charnock's opinion he was more useful in London and in particular to him personally.

He had disliked Kathleen Rothbury from that moment, and he had always despised all the beautiful but empty-headed women whose only occupation was playing with fire, or rather with hearts, with often disastrous consequences for those who got burnt.

The mere fact that Lord Charnock had been unresponsive to the invitation in her eyes and appeared to deliberately avoid her made Kathleen Rothbury all the keener.

Only when she was forced to admit defeat did she tell herself that sooner or later she would get even with Lord Charnock and teach him the lesson he obviously deserved.

From her point of view she could think of nothing more annoying than to be saddled with a young girl on a long voyage, and as she returned to London she hoped he would find it an inconvenience but at the same time feel that he must not neglect what was an obvious duty.

Lord Charnock, however, had no intention of considering anything but his own comfort. He had a great deal of work to do and was, as it happened, annoyed at having to visit Russia at this particular moment.

It was only because the Foreign Secretary had pleaded with him to undertake a very difficult mission that he had reluctantly agreed to go to St. Petersburg.

"There is nobody but you whom I could trust with this," Lord Palmerston had said. "You know as well as I do what the Russians are like. Their spies are everywhere, and anything you say or even think will be reported to the Chief of Police. What is more, I am told the Tsar's Secret Police are now in absolute control, besides the fact that the Tsar himself is becoming more and more irrational."

"I have heard that," Lord Charnock said, "and God knows what will eventually happen in that country."

The Foreign Secretary sighed.

"As it is, the Tsar is loathed by the Army. He flies into fanatical rages at the least provocation and is severe, vindictive, and mean."

Lord Charnock nodded.

"I have heard that too, but I hoped it was exaggerated."

"I am afraid not," Lord Palmerton replied. "He has turned his vast Empire into a barracks, and to him Sovereignty is merely an extension of Army discipline."

Lord Charnock sighed.

"I was told that he wrote in a report: 'I cannot permit one single person to dare to defy my wishes the moment he has been made aware of them.'"

Lord Palmerston nodded.

"That is true. But his wishes, unfortunately, are eccentric, to say the least of it. He has imposed the wearing of uniforms on professors, students, engineers, and members of the Civil Service."

"It seems incredible!" Lord Charnock murmured.

"Only the Army has the right to wear moustaches," Lord Palmerston went on with a smile, "but all moustaches have to be black—if necessary, dyed!"

Both men laughed. Then Lord Charnock said:

"The Tsar is undoubtedly the most alarming Sovereign in Europe, and, as I have already told you, I have no wish to go to St. Petersburg."

"There is nobody else who would not be bamboozled, hoodwinked, or hypnotised by him."

Lord Charnock sighed again.

"Very well, but I shall make my visit as brief as possible."

"As long as it is successful, you can come back tomorrow."

"Thank you!" Lord Charnock said sarcastically, realising the enormity of the task ahead of him.

He gave orders now for his despatch-boxes, and there were quite a number of them, to be placed where he could keep his eye on them.

Everything they contained was in code. At the same time, he was well aware that the Russians were past-masters at breaking codes, and also at inspecting anything a visitor possessed even when he claimed Diplomatic Immunity.

As an experienced traveller, he made sure that those who travelled with him knew how to ensure his comfort.

His valet, who had been with him for fifteen years, gave the stewards orders so that almost like magic everything was done in a manner which would have been the envy of other, less competent passengers.

Now as the ship began to move, Lord Charnock opened one of his despatch-boxes and started to work on what it contained.

He had not given one more thought to the responsibility the Countess of Rothbury had thrust upon him in the shape of her niece.

Chapter Two

Zelina felt very shy when it was time to go down to dinner.

However, when she entered the Dining-Saloon and gave a steward her name, she found that he escorted her not to the large table in the centre of the room, which was already nearly full, but to one of the single tables that were arranged round the walls.

She realised this had been arranged for her by the Russian Embassy and was grateful that she did not have to talk to the strangers, some of whom looked rather rough and became very noisy as the meal proceeded.

She had been eating for a short while when she saw Lord Charnock come into the Saloon, looking, she thought, very tall and disdainful of everybody and the surroundings in which he found himself.

He was escorted to a table at the far end which was in a small alcove, and therefore in a way he was isolated from contact with the other passengers.

Zelina could see him ordering his meal with care, and she noticed that a bottle of champagne in an ice-bucket was placed beside him.

He then opened a book which he had brought with him and started to read.

Immediately Zelina thought this was a wise thing to do and wished she had thought of it herself.

Because she was alone it was difficult not to stare at other people, and she knew that Lord Charnock had given her an idea as to how to occupy herself at the other meals when she would be sitting alone.

There were long pauses between the courses as there appeared not to be enough stewards to cater for all the demands of those having dinner.

Those at the centre table were continually asking for more wine and Zelina was sincerely grateful that she did not have to sit amongst them.

There was one man who was facing her from the other side of the table, and as the dinner progressed she was aware that he was looking at her in what she felt was an impertinent manner.

She wished that she could hurry away, but she thought it would only draw attention to herself if she left before the end of the meal.

She was in fact quite thankful when the last course was put in front of her and the steward asked her when it was finished if she required anything more.

"No, thank you," Zelina replied.

She rose from the table, and, walking gracefully but carefully because there was a decided roll, she went up the stairway and back to her own cabin.

It was quite a comfortable one, and she was glad that she had a book to read.

She would have liked to have taken more books for the voyage, but her aunt's lady's-maid who had helped her pack had insisted on filling her travelling-case to the brim with clothes.

"You don't know what you'll need, Miss, going to them foreign parts," she had said ominously. "From all I hears, it's always snowing in Russia."

"Not at this time of the year, I hope!" Zelina had said with a smile.

"You can't be certain, Miss," the maid had replied.

She obviously looked on Russia as a very outlandish place, and Zelina was inclined to agree with her.

Then she told herself that she had to be sensible,

and if she had to visit Russia then she must learn about its history and of course appreciate the treasures that every book told her she would find there.

But, however hard she tried to force herself into being excited at what lay ahead, she was still apprehensive and afraid.

The wind increased during the night, and by the morning when the ship was not pitching and tossing it was rolling uncomfortably.

Fortunately Zelina was a good sailor, and, finding her cabin rather hot and stifling, she put on her travelling-cape and went up on deck.

There were very few people about, and she realised it would be dangerous to walk any distance. She therefore stayed watching the white-crested waves from the shelter of a doorway.

The sea looked magnificent and Zelina was not afraid, except that she might get wet from the spray breaking over the deck.

She stood there for a long time, then as she turned to go inside she almost bumped into the man who had been staring at her from the centre table in the Dining-Saloon.

"Good-morning, pretty lady!" he said. "You're obviously a good sailor!"

"Good-morning!" Zelina answered politely, and tried to pass him.

However, he stood in her way and said:

"I looked for you last night after dinner but you'd disappeared."

Zelina wondered what she should say to avoid being friendly with him.

She thought it would seem too pompous to say that they had not been introduced. But she knew that he was the type of man her father would not have considered a gentleman and that she should certainly not encourage him.

Moreover, she was aware that he was looking at her in the way that had made her feel uncomfortable the night before, and she tried to move forward, saying as she did so:

"Excuse me, I wish to go to my cabin."

"What's the hurry?" he asked. "Come and sit down somewhere and tell me about yourself."

"I . . . I am afraid I am too . . . busy," Zelina replied, and again tried to pass him.

He would have stopped her, but at that moment one of the other passengers came through the outer door, and as he pushed by, Zelina followed him and escaped.

When she reached her cabin she found that her heart was beating fast and told herself it was stupid of her to be upset.

She thought it strange that her aunt had not sent a maid with her. Her mother and father had never allowed her to travel anywhere unaccompanied.

However, Aunt Kathleen had said that the Russian Embassy was arranging the whole voyage, and Zelina had imagined that in that case they would provide some sort of Chaperone for her.

She supposed now that while she was in a British ship she would hardly come under their jurisdiction and she would have to wait until she reached Stockholm before the Russians, so to speak, "took over."

She found horrifying the idea that all through the voyage she would have to avoid the man with the moustache.

Then she asked herself how he could hurt her, and she knew that now that she was grown up and on her own, she must learn to handle people without relying on her father as she had in the past.

Nevertheless, she felt very young and lost, and only by reading a book that she had brought with her and forcing herself to concentrate on it could she forget her feelings.

They ran into an even rougher sea before luncheon and in consequence there were few people in the Dining-Saloon. Amongst those missing was the man with the moustache, and Zelina gave a sigh of relief when he did not appear.

This time she had the foresight to take her book with her, and she noticed that Lord Charnock at the far end of the Saloon was also reading as he ate.

Because his eyes were on his book, Zelina was able to watch him for a little while and thought as she had before that he looked aloof and inhuman.

She guessed, because of the despatch-cases that had been carried aboard with him, that he had something to do with the Diplomatic Service and she wished she could talk to him about his work and ask him about Russia.

'If Papa were with me it would be so easy,' she thought, 'and I would like to hear more about the political situation in the country.'

Because she was thinking of Lord Charnock she was looking at him, and as if he was suddenly aware of it he raised his head from his book and looked directly at her.

Quickly she looked away, but the mere movement of her head attracted his attention, and, although she was unaware of it, the light coming through one of the port-holes glinted on her fair hair and gave her what appeared in the distance to be a halo.

Vaguely at the back of his mind Lord Charnock thought that she looked attractive, and then he wondered that such a young woman should be travelling alone.

It was merely a passing thought, and he was just about to look down again at his book when it struck him that the woman in question must be the Countess's niece.

He had not actually looked at her when the Countess asked him to take care of her during the voyage, because he had been so annoyed by the request.

Now it struck him as rather strange that a girl should be travelling alone, and he wondered why she should be going to Russia.

Then he told himself that it was not his concern, and if she was anything like her aunt he had no intention even of speaking to her.

However, he noticed that as soon as she finished her meal she picked up her book and walked quickly out of the Saloon.

'At least she is a good sailor!' he thought.

Lord Charnock spent that afternoon working. Then as it was impossible to walk round the deck because of the roughness of the sea, he spent a short time on the bridge with the Captain, a privilege accorded to him because of his importance and the fact that he was extremely interested in ships and was considering buying a yacht of his own.

By dinner-time the waves had subsided a little and a following wind was moving the ship quickly towards the shelter of the Danish coast.

When he had changed into his evening-clothes just as he would have changed whether he was at home or at Buckingham Palace, Lord Charnock went down to the Dining-Saloon knowing that he would be offered much the same menu as he had the night before.

There was still a distinct shortage of other diners, but Zelina on entering the Saloon five minutes earlier could see with a sense of foreboding that the man with the moustache was back in the same place he had occupied the night before.

Some men-friends were with him but there were no women, and they were obviously treating any queasy feelings they might have from the movement of the sea with wine.

Zelina did not look in their direction but she heard them shouting at the waiters to bring bottle after bottle, and halfway through the meal a steward came to Zelina's side to say:

"Mr. Adamson, Miss, asks if you'll take a glass of wine with him."

"Mr. Adamson?" Zelina repeated, not understanding what she was being offered.

Then as the steward glanced towards the centre table she knew who he was.

"Please thank the gentleman and say the answer is 'no'!" she said firmly.

"Thank you, Miss."

The steward relayed her answer, and then to Zelina's consternation Mr. Adamson rose somewhat unsteadily to his feet and shouted:

"If you won't join me, I drink to you, pretty lady! Good health!"

The ship rolled as he spoke, and while much of the wine in his glass splashed over onto the table, the other men laughed uproariously and put up their hands to support him.

Zelina, feeling the whole episode was intolerable, picked up her book and ran from the Saloon.

After she had locked herself in her cabin, there was a knock on the door.

"What is . . . it?" she asked apprehensively.

"It's the stewardess, Miss."

She went to the door and unlocked it.

"A steward from the Dining-Saloon tells me you left without finishing your dinner. Is there anything I can get you?"

"How kind of you to think of it," Zelina answered, "but I have had quite enough."

"He tells me a gentleman was being impertinent, but you mustn't worry, Miss. They always drinks too much when the sea gets rough."

Zelina did not know what to reply, and after a moment the stewardess said:

"If there's anything you want later, Miss, you let me know."

"Thank you, but I am going to bed," Zelina replied.

She locked her door and, having got into bed, finished her book.

It was then that she realised that she would have nothing to read for the next two days, but she felt sure there would be some books on board.

＊　　　＊　　　＊

The next morning Zelina rose very early and went to the Purser's office to enquire if there was a Library on the ship.

She was told that there were a number of books in the Writing-Room but to be careful about returning them as a large number went missing on every voyage.

"Even the most respectable people become thieves when it is a question of a book," the Purser said with a smile.

"I expect what happens is that they get halfway through one and cannot bear not to know the ending!" Zelina said.

The Purser agreed, thinking that when she smiled Miss Tiverton was the prettiest girl he had ever seen in his whole life.

"Are you all right, Miss?" he asked. "I hear one of the passengers was being cheeky in the Saloon last night."

Zelina thought the ship was rather like a small village where everything was known the moment it happened.

"I am all right," she said, "but perhaps it might be wiser for me to have dinner in my cabin, if it is not inconvenient."

"I am afraid you'll find it rather uncomfortable and

cramped," the Purser said. "But don't worry, I'll have a word with the gentleman in question and tell him to behave himself."

"I would not wish you to do that," Zelina said quickly.

"You leave everything to me," the Purser said in a fatherly manner. "We're here to look after our passengers and see to their comfort. If you were my daughter I'd be worried about you travelling alone."

"It is the first time I have done so," Zelina replied.

"Well, if you are at all upset by anything, you come and tell me," the Purser answered, "and what happened last night, I promise you, will not happen again."

"Thank you," Zelina said.

Because he had been so kind, she felt a new warmth inside her as she went in search of the Writing-Room.

There were two large bookcases filled with books, most of them appearing to be rather dull. But there was one on Russia, which she took from the shelf to carry back to her cabin.

It was a short book but very interesting, describing various parts of the country, the Churches in Moscow, and the Palaces in St. Petersburg. Unfortunately, because it was so short she had finished it by five o'clock in the evening.

She thought this would be a good time to get some fresh air. Although she had no idea how men like Mr. Adamson behaved, she knew there was a Smoking-Room on board, as it was marked on the plan of the ship which was in her cabin, and she had the idea that he and his rowdy friends would be sitting there.

She therefore went on deck on the other side of the ship and sat looking at the sea and breathing the fresh air.

Even though it was cold she felt that it was invigorating, and only when she felt she should be changing for dinner did she go inside.

*   *   *

Lord Charnock had also thought that late in the afternoon would be a good time to take some exercise, and, having walked the deck for nearly half-an-hour, he was ready to return to his cabin.

He was an active man and when he was on dry land he rode every day of his life.

He preferred galloping over his own Park-land at Charnock Park, where he had a stable of outstanding horses, many of which he had bred himself.

In London he always rode very early in the morning when the Park was not crowded, and, rather than the fashionable Rotten Row, he preferred the less-frequented parts where he could give his horse its head.

He hoped he would have time to ride in Russia, feeling that otherwise he would be stifled in the overheated Palaces. At the same time, he was well aware that the distance he would have to travel to get from one place to another was the equivalent of several miles' walk in England.

He sighed as he thought of how many corridors he would have to traverse and the many long-winded interviews he would have to endure.

However optimistic Lord Palmerston might be, there was every likelihood that his mission would be a failure.

Then he told himself that he seldom failed. In fact it was a word he disliked and was sure should not be in his vocabulary.

Nobody looking at him with his enigmatic, indifferent, expressionless face would have realised that underneath the façade he offered to the world Lord Charnock had a great sense of adventure.

He loved the cut and thrust of diplomatic intrigue, which was as thrilling to him as was a battle to a dedicated soldier or a kill to a big-game hunter.

On this trip to Russia he was pitting his own brain against the brains of the most skilful and perhaps the most sinister men in the whole world of politics.

There were a thousand questions that every Diplomat wished to know about the intentions of the Tsar, and because he was such an unpredictable character, it was extremely difficult even to guess what line he might take towards a number of other European nations apart from his intervention in Turkey.

When Lord Charnock thought of what lay ahead of him when he reached St. Petersburg, he was almost appalled at the enormity of the difficulties he had to face.

Then with a faint twist of his lips he told himself that however devious or unpredictable the Russians might be, he would eventually get the better of them, if only because some inner strength gave him the power to do so.

It was not a thing that he could talk about, but he was aware that he had a perception which often revealed to him what another man was thinking or, better still, what he was hiding.

It was not a power he used every day, but in an emergency it was there if he called upon it, and it was a reassurance which he thought to himself was more comforting than was a massive reinforcement of troops to a General battling against superior odds.

He had left the deck and was walking along the corridor to his own cabin when he heard a sudden scream.

For a moment he thought he had been mistaken, then he heard the scream again.

As he looked round and wondered where it had come from, he realised he was outside the Writing-Room. Then he heard a woman's voice say:

"Go . . . away! Leave me . . . alone!"

"That's something I have no intention of doing, pretty lady!"

As the man's voice spoke the last two words, Lord Charnock remembered that he had heard them spoken at dinner last night.

He had not missed the noisy toast shouted across the cabin by a drunken man, and it was only as the woman he had addressed had run up the stairs that he had realised it was the Countess's young niece.

It had flashed through his mind then that he should do something about it, but when she disappeared he told himself that the best thing to do was to pretend he had not seen what had happened.

Now, without thinking or considering that he had no wish to be involved, Lord Charnock opened the door of the Writing-Room and walked in.

One glance told him what was going on.

Zelina was standing with her back to the bookcase, struggling against the man who had toasted her last night, who was now obviously attempting to kiss her.

The noise Lord Charnock made opening the door made him turn his head, and in that moment Zelina was free of him and ran across the room.

"Please stop . . . him!" she begged Lord Charnock in a terrified voice. "Please . . . do not . . . let him . . . touch me!"

Lord Charnock was looking at the man in a way which would have made one of his own class quail.

"Get out of here!" he said in a voice that sounded like the crack of a whip. "I shall report your behaviour to the Captain and advise him to have you confined to your cabin for the rest of the voyage!"

Adamson opened his mouth to speak, then thought better of it and walked past Lord Charnock without looking at him.

Only when the door was closed behind him did Zelina, who was trembling, say:

"Thank you . . . thank you . . . he . . . frightened me."

"Sit down for a moment," Lord Charnock said.

Because she felt that if she did not do so she might actually fall down, Zelina obeyed.

She sat on a hard chair, and when her face was raised to his he saw by the darkness in her eyes and the trembling of her hands that she was in fact very frightened.

Lord Charnock sat down beside her and asked:

"Why is your maid not with you? Surely you are not travelling alone?"

"I . . . I am . . . alone."

She saw the surprise in his eyes and added:

"Everything was . . . arranged by the Russian . . . Embassy . . . and I think perhaps Aunt Kathleen thought . . . as I did . . . that they would send . . . somebody to be with me."

Lord Charnock thought it was what anyone might have expected, but the Countess either had not taken the trouble to enquire into the arrangements made for her niece, or else was too mean to pay the fare for a lady's-maid.

Aloud he said:

"You are certainly too young to be travelling alone."

He nearly added: ". . . and too pretty," but he was aware that that would frighten Zelina even more.

"It was . . . stupid of me not to stay in my . . . cabin after the way he . . . behaved last night," Zelina said in a hesitating little voice, "but the Purser told me it would not . . . happen again."

"I am afraid that is the sort of thing you might encounter on any ship if you travel alone," Lord Charnock remembered.

It sounded to Zelina as if he were reprimanding

her for being so foolish. She could think of nothing she could say in reply, and only bent her head as if she were a School-girl who was being reproved.

After a moment he asked:

"Why are you going to Russia?"

"Aunt Kathleen has . . . arranged for me to . . . stay with the Princess Volkonsky."

"In what capacity?"

"She was rather . . . vague about it . . . but I think I will be . . . expected to . . . teach her children to . . . speak English."

"Is that something you would like to do?"

There was a perceptible pause. Then, as if Zelina felt she must tell him the truth, she said:

"It is . . . something I had never . . . thought of doing . . . but my mother and father are dead . . . and Aunt Kathleen is . . . my Guardian."

She spoke quite simply and there was no need to elaborate any further. Lord Charnock was well aware that the Countess of Rothbury would have no wish to chaperone a niece, and certainly not such a pretty one.

He never listened to gossip if he could help it, but it was impossible not to be aware that the Countess's love-affair with Lord Merrihew was the talk of the Clubs.

Lord Charnock was fond of Harry Merrihew, but he was aware that he had an eye for any pretty woman who came in sight, and he was sure in consequence that the Countess had urgent personal reasons for sending Zelina as far away from London as possible.

"Had you ever thought of going to Russia?" he asked.

"It had never been a country which . . . Papa and I . . . wished to visit," Zelina answered, "but Aunt Kathleen thought it . . . appropriate because my Godmother was Russian, and I have a Russian name."

"What is it?"

"Zelina."

He thought again that Russia being farther from England than any other European country was the real reason for the Countess's choice.

"I am sure you will find it very interesting, once you get used to living there."

"I . . . hope so," Zelina said in a small voice. "That is why I was . . . trying to find some . . . books about it."

She looked towards the open bookcase as if to explain to Lord Charnock why she was in the Writing-Room in the first place.

"I cannot imagine there is anything of any great interest here," he said scornfully, "but as I have some books in my cabin, I will tell my valet to bring them to you, and I am sure you will find them informative, if somewhat difficult to read."

Zelina smiled and it swept away some of the fear in her face, and Lord Charnock realised that she was not trembling as violently as she had when she first sat down.

"Nothing is too hard for me to read," she said, "and thank you very much indeed for saying you will lend me your books. If you have one on politics, I would like that more than anything else."

Lord Charnock raised his eye-brows.

"Politics?" he enquired.

"Papa explained to me about the Prussian occupation of Poland and the trouble in Turkey three years ago. I thought then how clever Lord Palmerston was."

"He is indeed," Lord Charnock agreed.

He was exceedingly surprised that Zelina was interested in such things, finding usually that women, especially if they were pretty, found politics a bore.

However, he had no intention of discussing such matters with a girl who might repeat or twist what he said, and he therefore rose to his feet, saying as he did so:

"If you feel better now, Miss Tiverton, I will escort you back to your cabin, and I suggest that as you have had an uncomfortable experience it would be wise for you to have dinner there tonight."

"I meant to do that anyway," Zelina replied, "and if I could have something to read I would not need to be seen until we reach Stockholm."

"Stockholm?" Lord Charnock questioned.

"That is where I change onto a Russian ship."

She looked up at him and asked:

"Are you getting off before that?"

Even as she spoke, she thought that what she was implying was an imposition.

At the same time, she could not bear to think that if any further unpleasantness arose with Mr. Adamson, Lord Charnock would not be on board.

She had never dreamt, had never imagined, that she would be involved with a man like Adamson and with nobody to turn to for protection.

Now she thought frantically that she would lock herself in her cabin and stay there until the moment came when she must transfer to the Russian ship.

Then it flashed through her mind that there would probably be other men of the same type in that ship, and if they were Russian instead of English, it might be even worse.

As she was thinking she had no idea how revealing her eyes were, or perhaps because Lord Charnock was perceptive he was aware that her fears were mounting.

He thought for a moment. Then he said:

"Actually, I am getting off at Copenhagen."

Zelina realised that when he did so there was still the voyage up the Baltic to Stockholm, and she supposed that Mr. Adamson would still be aboard.

She was silent for a moment. Then she said:

"I have . . . no right to ask you this . . . but could

you please . . . find out if that . . . man is . . . leaving the ship at Copenhagen or travelling to . . . Stockholm?"

Then, as if it was difficult to speak as calmly as she was doing, she added frantically:

"Y-you do not think he will . . . be going to . . . St. Petersburg?"

"I will find out where he is going," Lord Charnock promised, "and also make sure he behaves himself. I promise you the Captain will take a very serious view of men who thrust themselves on unprotected women, but you know as well as I do that you should not be alone."

He spoke sharply because it made him so angry that the Countess of Rothbury should have put her niece in such an incredibly vulnerable position and had tried to make him feel responsible for her.

Zelina heard the anger in his voice and saw it in his face.

"I am . . . sorry . . . very sorry to be such a . . . nuisance," she said. "Please . . . forgive me . . . and I will try not to . . . b-bother you . . . again."

The way she spoke and the fact that the fear was back in her eyes made Lord Charnock feel that he was being cruel to something small and defenceless.

"I told you to leave this to me," he said, "and I think, if you will honour me by dining with me this evening, it will make it quite clear to that very unpleasant man that you are under my protection. In which case I am quite certain he will not interfere with you again."

"Can I . . . do that?" Zelina asked in a low voice. "Do you . . . mean it?"

"I shall be delighted for you to do so, and perhaps I will be able to tell you something of what you want to know about Russia."

Zelina drew in her breath, and Lord Charnock saw

that the stricken look had gone from her eyes and instead they were shining.

"It is very . . . very kind of you," she said, "but you are . . . quite certain I will not be a bother . . . and you would not rather read your book than talk to me?"

Lord Charnock smiled.

"If we bore each other," he said, "we can both read our books. So bring yours with you, but I doubt if reading it will be necessary."

"I do hope not!"

Because she spoke so fervently he laughed.

"I think we can dine a little later than usual," he said, "and hope the more rowdy elements amongst the passengers will have nearly finished their meal. I will wait for you in the Saloon at quarter-to-eight."

"Thank you . . . thank you . . . very much!" Zelina said.

*   *   *

Zelina took a great deal of trouble in arranging her hair when she dressed for dinner.

Her aunt's maid had packed only three rather simple evening-gowns for the voyage, saying that her best ones should not be worn until she reached St. Petersburg.

Even so, they were expensive gowns which had come from Bond Street, and in Zelina's eyes they were so beautiful that she was almost afraid to touch them.

When her aunt had seemed so kind in buying them for her, she had had no idea that she was doing so because she was sending her away, and in fact had provided her with enough clothing to last for a year or more.

But whatever the reason, it was a relief to think that in St. Petersburg she would not feel like a beggar-maid or be treated as one.

She was not quite sure if in Russian eyes she would

be nothing but a Governess, whose treatment in English houses was something which had aroused her mother's compassion.

"Poor creature!" she had said once when they had heard their hostess being rude to the Governess who looked after the children.

"Surely it is wrong for any lady to speak like that to somebody who cannot answer back?" Zelina had said at the time.

"Governesses have a particularly bad time of it because they are between the devil and the deep blue sea," her mother had replied.

Zelina looked at her mother for an explanation and she said:

"They are not considered the equal of their employers but are a cut above the other servants. They are therefore in a world of their own, with few privileges, and I always feel very sorry for them."

After that Zelina had always gone out of her way to speak to the Governesses at the houses they visited, and she knew they were grateful for any attention they might receive.

That, she thought, was the position in which she would find herself. It was a frightening thought and a humiliating one.

Then she decided that if it was too unbearable she would go home, and once she was back there would be nothing Aunt Kathleen could do about it.

When she was finally dressed and looked in the mirror, she did not look in the least like a Governess.

In fact, she thought, she might be going off to her first fashionable Ball, which would be an excitement she had never known.

She could not help feeling a little sad that while she was in London she had never had the chance even of seeing one of the Balls that were described in the *Ladies Journal* as being so spectacular.

She had often imagined beautiful women like her aunt dancing under chandeliers lit with hundreds of tapers while a Band played romantic tunes.

The floor would be filled with elegant gentlemen dancing with ladies who in their full gowns looked like swans as they moved over the polished floor.

'Perhaps even in Russia I shall not be asked to a Ball,' Zelina thought despondently.

Then she told herself that she would not speculate about what lay in the future but would enjoy tonight because she was dining with a man who had the answers to many of the questions that puzzled her.

She was afraid of being in the Saloon too early and having to wait alone, but when she reached it Lord Charnock was there, looking extremely smart in his evening-clothes but somehow more awe-inspiring than he had been in the afternoon.

Zelina curtseyed to him and he said:

"I am sure by this time you are hungry. I have a feeling that as the food will not be very palatable, our conversation must be a recompense for it."

"That is what I am looking forward to," Zelina said, "and I am sure that when you talk about the things I want to hear, the food will taste like ambrosia."

"I only hope you will not be disappointed."

He spoke in such a dry way that it made Zelina wonder nervously if she had been too enthusiastic, and she told herself humbly that she must behave in a very circumspect manner since he was being so kind in letting her dine with him when she was quite certain he would rather read his book.

When they appeared together in the Dining-Saloon Zelina was aware that there was a sudden hush amongst the other diners, and every head was turned in their direction.

She did not look, but she was quite certain that Mr. Adamson would get the message that Lord Charnock intended to protect her and he would not dare approach her again.

They reached the alcove where there were two stewards waiting to assist them to their chairs, and there was a bottle of champagne on ice.

When the food came, Zelina was certain that it was not the meal she would have been eating if she had been at her own table.

Instead, they started with caviar, then there were other dishes which, while she found them delicious, Lord Charnock ate without comment.

They talked, and she was delighted that at last she had found somebody to tell her a little about Russia.

She was intelligent enough to realise that everything Lord Charnock said was somehow impersonal and could have been printed in a Guide-Book without anybody questioning its source.

Yet she found it fascinating to listen to his description of the building of St. Petersburg when the Capital should really have been situated in another part of Russia where the climate was more salubrious.

"Tsar Peter was a fantastic character," Lord Charnock said, "and although you will find St. Petersburg itself an awe-inspiring city, it is difficult to forget that the historians claim that two-hundred-thousand people died in twenty years while the city was being constructed."

Zelina gave an exclamation of horror and he continued:

"While labourers were recruited from all parts of Europe, wages were not paid, desertion was chronic, and sickness festered and death battered in that delta-marsh with the Neva constantly in flood."

Lord Charnock realised as he spoke that he was painting a picture that to Zelina was as vivid as if she saw it happening before her very eyes.

He found it a compliment he had not enjoyed before to be with a woman who was so absorbed by what he was saying that he was aware that she did not think of him as a man but almost as if he were an oracle.

He went on to explain how occasionally the slaves rebelled, while the Tsar, living for years in a small log-cabin consisting of three rooms, flung himself into activities which ranged from personally hammering out sheets of iron weighing hundreds of pounds to performing an operation on a woman suffering from dropsy.

"Was he really mad?" Zelina asked.

"No—Russian!" Lord Charnock replied. "His reforms and innovations are impressive. He built up heavy industry in the Urals, founded Military and Naval Colleges, Schools for engineers, introduced the first newspapers, the first public Theatre, and the first Hospital."

"He sounds quite fantastic!" Zelina exclaimed.

"But the bonds of serfdom were tight," Lord Charnock went on. "The nobility lost its last thread of independence and the Tsar allowed no man to possess anything that he could call his own."

They talked until they were the last people left in the Dining-Saloon.

When Zelina realised that they must leave, she said in a voice that vibrated with sincerity:

"Thank you! Thank you! I cannot tell you how wonderful it has been for me to listen to you and to learn so much. You have been very, very kind."

"I too have enjoyed the evening," Lord Charnock replied. "I hope I can persuade you to dine with me tomorrow."

He did not miss the excitement in Zelina's eyes.

"You are quite . . . certain you will not find it a . . . bore?" she asked.

"I am being selfish in admitting that I would not ask you unless I wanted you to accept."

"Thank you. It is something to which I shall look forward all day, even when I am reading your books."

They left the Dining-Saloon together, and when they reached the deck above, Zelina curtseyed.

"Thank you a thousand times, My Lord, for the most exciting evening I have ever spent!"

She walked away towards her cabin without waiting for his reply.

He thought as he watched her go that never before had he met a woman who did not try to stay with him for a little while longer or had been so attentive to anything he might say.

"She is certainly different from her aunt!" he told himself.

Then as he went to his own cabin he was thinking about the amount of work that was waiting for him there.

Chapter Three

"I hear, My Lord," the Captain said, "that you're thinking of leaving us at Copenhagen."

"I am," Lord Charnock agreed. "His Imperial Majesty is sending the Royal Yacht *Ischora* for me."

"It's an honour," the Captain remarked briefly.

He was silent for a moment and Lord Charnock realised he was debating in his mind what he wanted to say.

They were passing through the narrow strait between Denmark and Sweden, with beautiful scenery on each side, and out of the wind the ship was moving smoothly and comparatively fast without the need of her auxiliary sails.

"I'm worried, My Lord," the Captain said at last, "about Miss Tiverton, who I understand is travelling with us as far as Stockholm."

"So she informs me," Lord Charnock replied coldly.

He wondered why the Captain should take it upon himself to discuss Zelina with him, but his next words were very revealing.

"I understand from the Purser that you saved Miss Tiverton, My Lord, from an uncomfortable situation with one of the passengers."

"I was going to report it to you myself," Lord Charnock replied, "but I made it clear that if the man in question continued to annoy the young lady, he would be dealt with not only by you but also by me!"

"Your methods were obviously very effective, My Lord," the Captain said, "but I'm apprehensive as to what'll happen when you leave us."

Lord Charnock did not reply and there was a scowl on his forehead.

He resented being made responsible for Zelina and he thought it an impertinence for the Captain to speak in this way.

"I can deal with Mr. Adamson and his like when they're English," the Captain went on, "but at Copenhagen we often have a number of young officers come aboard to travel with us as far as Stockholm. They're young and they enjoy themselves in their own way. But Your Lordship'll understand that a beautiful young woman travelling alone will be a heavy responsibility."

Lord Charnock was instantly aware of what the Captain was insinuating by rather devious means.

He told himself that he had no intention of taking Zelina with him on the Royal yacht. At the same time, he realised that when he left the English ship her position could be intolerable.

He knew what young Army officers from any country could be like when they were off-duty and determined to enjoy themselves before they reached another Barracks where they would again be under Military discipline.

As he thought about it he realised how hopelessly inadequate Zelina was to deal with a situation which would almost inevitably arise because she was so unusually attractive.

The night that she had dined with him he had found that she was intelligent and unusually well read, but he was well aware that she was also completely innocent.

He found himself growing more and more angry that Kathleen Rothbury should have dared to send a girl who in some ways was as helpless as a child on a trip which might have been difficult enough for a very much older and experienced woman.

Only yesterday he had had an example of Zelina's innocence, and he knew that any outsider would have put a very different construction upon it.

When they were finishing dinner Zelina had said:

"I so much enjoyed the book you lent me and, although it seems greedy, I hope you have another I may borrow."

"You have finished that one already?" he had asked in surprise.

"I read very quickly."

"You must do, but fortunately I have quite a considerable library with me."

Her eyes lit up as if he had given her a present of inestimable value, and she said:

"You are so kind! Shall I bring the book I have finished to your cabin?"

It flashed through Lord Charnock's mind that that was the sort of suggestion her aunt might have made or any other woman who was seeking to attract him physically.

Then as he looked into Zelina's eyes he knew that she was so unversed in the ways of the Social World that she had no idea that she had suggested something preposterous.

"I will send my valet to your cabin after dinner," he had replied, "with a book which I am sure you will enjoy reading. He can also collect the one you have finished."

"Thank you very much," Zelina had answered, "but I have no wish to cause you so much trouble."

Lord Charnock considered for a moment whether he should warn her that another man in his position might have taken advantage of her suggestion.

Then he told himself that it would only make her

self-conscious, and perhaps the mere fact that she was so ingenuous would be a protection in itself.

At the same time, he doubted it, especially in Russia.

Now he knew that it would be impossible for him, as a gentleman or as a man with any human feeling, to leave Zelina to travel on alone to Stockholm with a shipload of rowdy young officers and the man Adamson, who had already tried to force his attentions on her.

Stiffly, because he could also see that damaging insinuations might be made concerning his interference, he said:

"I am glad you mentioned this to me, Captain. I shall most certainly consider what should be done about Miss Tiverton, and I will discuss it with the British Minister Plenipotentiary at Copenhagen, Sir Henry Watkin Williams-Winn, who will doubtless be coming aboard on my arrival."

"Thank you, My Lord," the Captain said. "You've certainly taken a great weight off my shoulders."

To his own annoyance, because it interfered with his work, Lord Charnock found himself thinking about Zelina during the afternoon.

When they met at dinner he realised that she was longing to talk to him about the book he had loaned her.

"It is extremely interesting," she said, "especially where it refers to the Russians' policy in regard to Poland, but I do not think it is quite honest about what happened there."

Lord Charnock looked at her in surprise.

"What do you mean by that?"

"I have only just remembered, because it was some years ago, what I read at the time of their cruelty when they abducted one-hundred-thousand Polish children from their parents and sent them to the interior of Russia."

Lord Charnock sipped the champagne which had been poured out for him and wondered what he should reply.

He had in fact been appalled and horrified at the reports of the Russian atrocities, and he had joined with the Radicals in Parliament in urging Lord Palmerston to make the strongest protest possible about it to the Tsar.

He had been amongst those who had been indignant that Lord Palmerston had defended the Russians by referring to the debt Europe owed them for driving back Napoleon's invasion of their country.

When he did not speak, Zelina said in a voice that vibrated with feeling:

"I read a speech made in the House of Commons which described the children screaming as they were taken away from Warsaw, while their mothers hurled themselves on the railway-line in an attempt to stop the departing trains."

She looked at Lord Charnock as she spoke, and he could see the horror in her expression before she added:

"How can I even . . . consider being . . . friends with people who . . . behaved like . . . that?"

There was a pause before Lord Charnock said:

"I want to talk to you about your visit to Russia, but I suggest that we first have something to eat and discuss a more cheerful subject than the one you have introduced so early in the meal."

Zelina thought he was rebuking her and she blushed.

"I am . . . sorry," she said humbly.

Lord Charnock talked about Denmark, saying that it was a pity she would not be able to see the Danish cottages, which were only of one storey but were large and immensely high.

Because she found that anything he said was interesting, Zelina listened to him attentively until the coffee which ended the meal was poured out and Lord Charnock ordered a brandy for himself.

Then as the Dining-Saloon was emptying and it was easier to speak in a quieter voice, he said:

"What I want to discuss with you is your visit to St. Petersburg."

He saw an expression of apprehension sweep away the eagerness on Zelina's face as he said:

"You told me, the first night we talked together, that your aunt was rather vague about what you should do when you get there."

"She would not answer my questions . . . directly," Zelina replied, "but I am sure she . . . intends me to be a . . . Governess to the Princess's children."

"In fact, if that is true," Lord Charnock said, "it is not quite the same subservient position as it would be in an English household."

Zelina looked at him enquiringly and he said:

"Two years ago Prince Khristofor de Lieven, who had been Russian Ambassador in England for many years and whose wife was one of the acknowledged leaders of London Society, was recalled to his own country to become Governor and Tutor to the Tsarevitch."

"Can that be true?" Zelina exclaimed in surprise.

"I assure you I am usually extremely accurate in any statement I make," Lord Charnock answered.

She flushed and said quickly:

"I did not mean to be rude . . . but all the Governesses I have known have always been rather . . . crushed creatures who seemed almost . . . apologetic at being . . . alive."

"I thought that was what you were thinking," Lord Charnock said, "and that is why you must make sure that does not happen to you."

"But how can I prevent it?" Zelina asked.

Lord Charnock sat back a little more comfortably in his chair, his glass in his hand.

"The Russian aristocrats," he said, "are what you and I would call 'snobs,' and they appreciate only what they consider the best and most expensive."

Zelina looked puzzled and he went on:

"If you approach them humbly and they find you are subservient, then they will doubtless treat you as they treat their own people, with contempt and indifference."

As he spoke the last words he thought that he was being a little too outspoken, and he added quickly:

"What I am suggesting is that you show the Princess from the very beginning that you come from a distinguished English family and you are therefore the equal of anybody in Russia, except perhaps the Royal Family."

Zelina drew in her breath.

"I understand what you are . . . saying, but how can I make them think I am of any . . . importance when I arrive . . . unchaperoned, and I am, as far as I know, engaged by the Princess to . . . attend only to her . . . children?"

Lord Charnock thought it was quite quick of Zelina to have worked this out for herself, and aloud he said firmly:

"That is the impression you must destroy immediately on arrival."

"But . . . how? How?" Zelina asked.

"That is what I am going to tell you," he said, "and the first person I intend to discuss this with is the British Minister in Copenhagen."

"Where you . . . leave the . . . ship," Zelina murmured almost beneath her breath.

"Which I intend that you should do too," Lord Charnock said.

"You . . . mean I can . . . come with you?"

He thought the light that appeared in her eyes was almost dazzling, and he asked:

"You knew I was leaving?"

"Yes, indeed, your valet told me that the Tsar was sending his own private yacht for you."

"That is true," Lord Charnock replied, thinking he must tell Hibbert in future to keep his mouth shut.

It was unlike the man to be talkative, but he was quite certain that because Zelina was so much alone and also so curious about what was happening, she had plied his servant with questions, being well aware how frightening it would be when he left the ship.

"What I intend to tell Sir Henry Watkin Williams-Winn," Lord Charnock said, "is that the Chaperone arranged for you by your aunt was taken seriously ill at the very last moment before the ship left. She must in fact have had food-poisoning, because her maid was incapacitated in the same way at the same time."

He paused, then went on slowly, as if thinking out the plan.

"Because it was impossible for her to travel, out of the kindness of your heart you left your own lady's-maid to attend to her and were therefore left to travel alone to Russia."

Zelina listened wide-eyed.

"And will Sir Henry . . . believe that . . . story?"

"He will believe me."

"Yes . . . yes . . . of course, and I must tell the same . . . tale when I . . . arrive . . . in St. Petersburg."

"Naturally," Lord Charnock agreed, "and as neither Sir Henry nor I can allow a young English lady to travel alone to Stockholm and certainly not on a Russian ship, we will arrange for you to transfer to the Royal Yacht *Ischora*."

Zelina clasped her hands together.

"How can you be so . . . kind . . . so wonderful to . . . me? I was very . . . very frightened as to what would . . . happen when I was . . . alone."

Lord Charnock knew she was thinking of the man Adamson, and he said sharply:

"Forget him! And tell nobody you have been insulted in such a manner. They would not be at all sorry for you but merely shocked that you should be in such an invidious position, which would reflect on your social status."

Zelina nodded and Lord Charnock went on:

"When you arrive in St. Petersburg you will make it obvious to the Princess the moment that you have come as a guest and that being employed in any capacity had never so much as entered your mind."

"How . . . can I do that?" Zelina enquired.

"First, you will thank Her Highness for inviting you to stay, saying how much you have looked forward to seeing Russia because your Godmother was a Russian."

Lord Charnock paused.

"You did say that was the reason for your name?"

Zelina nodded.

"My Godmother was the Countess Zelina Trubensov."

"I know the family," Lord Charnock said. "And who was your father?"

"My father was a Major in the Life Guards which my grandfather commanded at one time."

"What was his name?"

"General Sir Edward Tiverton."

Lord Charnock smiled.

"That will certainly impress the Tsar, who has an obsession for anything Military!"

"The . . . Tsar?"

As Zelina asked the question she could not imagine how she would be of any interest to the Tsar.

"One thing you have not been told," Lord Charnock replied, "is that your host, Prince Ivan Volkonsky, is the younger brother of Prince Peter, who is the most senior officer at the Imperial Court. If you are a *guest* of the Princess, you will undoubtedly meet His Imperial Majesty quite frequently."

Zelina looked startled. At the same time, she had not missed the accent Lord Charnock had put on the word "guest."

"Now, as a guest," he went on, "you will, when you arrive, present your hostess with a gift. That is something which is usual in foreign countries but would not be thought of by anybody in a servile position."

"What . . . shall I . . . give her?" Zelina asked.

"Something small that would not be in the least pretentious. I am sure you have something of the sort with you: a scarf, a silk or lace handkerchief, or a fan."

"Yes, of course I have things like that," Zelina said, remembering all the purchases her aunt had made, many of which, she had thought, would never be of any use to her.

"That is the start," Lord Charnock said. "Then, remember that your uncle and aunt are extremely important members of the British aristocracy, and you must behave in the same manner as you think they would in the same circumstances."

As he spoke he thought cynically that the last thing Zelina should do was to behave like her aunt, but he knew that she had no idea how Kathleen Rothbury would have behaved had she been unaccompanied on the ship with him.

Zelina had never shown in any way that she thought of him as an attractive man, nor had she made any effort to draw his attention to herself as a woman.

She listened to him wide-eyed and attentively, she asked his opinions, and, Lord Charnock realised, she had done everything possible to "pick his brains."

But they had all been impersonal conversations such as he might easily have had with a man or one of the older and intelligent women who, in London, still had an unassailable place in the Social World.

He saw that Zelina was thinking over what he had said to her, and after a moment she said:

"How can I ... thank you for being so ... kind and ... understanding? Now I know exactly what I must do ... and I only hope I am intelligent and capable enough to do it."

"Of course you are!" he said reassuringly. "And there is something else, Zelina, that I wish to say to you."

Neither Zelina nor Lord Charnock noticed that he had used her Christian name as he continued:

"Russians have very fiery, impulsive temperaments. Unless you wish to be involved in situations which you will find embarrassing and perhaps frightening, you must try never, in any circumstances, to be alone with a Russian man!"

Again Zelina was surprised and in fact considerably startled.

She sat bolt upright and stared at Lord Charnock, and after a moment she said:

"Are you saying ... are you suggesting that if I was alone with him, a ... Russian might try to ... kiss me as that horrible ... common man was ... trying to do?"

"It would be quite a natural impulse on his part," Lord Charnock said drily.

"It is horrible ... terrifying!" Zelina said. "Last night I woke up screaming because I dreamt you had not rescued me."

"You must make sure it does not happen again."

"I thought it was ... just because he was such a ... vulgar type of person who had had too much to ... drink."

"Men are much the same all the world over," Lord Charnock said. "As I have told you, the Russians are very impulsive and they find a beautiful woman irresistible."

He had not meant to compliment Zelina openly,

but he saw her look at him incredulously. Then as her eye-lashes fluttered over her eyes, she said incoherently:

"I . . . I will try very . . . very hard not to be in such a . . . position."

She looked so young and so helpless as she spoke that Lord Charnock felt he could understand almost any man except himself wanting to put his arms round her and promise to protect her.

But that was something which he knew she would find very frightening, and he thought angrily that it would undoubtedly happen unless she was careful to follow his advice and arrange to be permanently chaperoned.

He thought that when he reached St. Petersburg he would have a word with the British Ambassador, the Earl of Durham, who could undoubtedly make clear what was Zelina's social position in England.

Then he told himself once again that he was becoming far too involved with this tiresome child, and it was all the more infuriating because it was obviously exactly what her aunt had intended when she had made him responsible for her.

'Dammit, Kathleen Rothbury has made a "cat's paw" of me,' he thought. 'If I had any sense, I would leave the girl to go to the devil in her own way!'

Then as if the violence of his feelings communicated itself to Zelina, she said in a frightened little voice:

"You are looking very . . . angry, and I am sure it is because I am being such a . . . trouble to you. If it is all too . . . difficult, I will go to Stockholm as arranged . . . and if I lock myself in my cabin nobody will be able to . . . get at me."

With an effort Lord Charnock drove the scowl from between his eyes.

"I am not angry with you," he answered, "but with your aunt. She had no right to put you in this position in the first place."

"I am sure she did not do it intentionally," Zelina said, "but Papa always said she was... frivolous and empty-headed and that was why he so seldom saw anything of her."

Lord Charnock thought it must have been a shock to Kathleen Rothbury when her niece had appeared.

"That is certainly a charitable way of looking at it," he said, "but remember what I told you, Zelina. This sort of situation must never occur again, and, however much you may be tempted, you are to stay with the Princess or some older woman wherever you may be. And do not believe half the compliments you will receive."

Zelina laughed, and it was a young, carefree sound.

"I think it doubtful I shall have any, but it would be very exciting if I did."

"That is just how you must not consider them," Lord Charnock insisted.

"I will try not to," Zelina answered, "and now that you have been so very clever in telling me what to do, I shall remember to myself that if I were just a poor, crushed, subservient Governess, nobody would even look at me."

Lord Charnock thought that was certainly untrue, but it was something he could not explain.

He could only hope that Zelina would follow his advice and most of all would not lose her heart to some young Russian who too late would make it clear that his intentions were strictly dishonourable.

"Thank you... thank you... for being so... wonderful and so very... very helpful," Zelina was saying.

*   *   *

As Lord Charnock had expected, the British Minister Plenipotentiary at Copenhagen was horrified to hear the chapter of accidents which had resulted in the niece of the Earl and Countess of Rothbury being alone on a

British ship and nearly being transferred, again alone, to a Russian vessel.

"This certainly must not happen, My Lord!" he said to Lord Charnock. "I will have a word with General Suchtelen, who is, I understand, waiting to welcome you aboard the *Ischora*."

"I believe I have met the General before," Lord Charnock said. "His father was, I think, the late Russian Minister to Stockholm."

"He was, and the General is a very intelligent man, so you should enjoy your sail through the Baltic."

"I am looking forward to it," Lord Charnock replied.

He went ashore with Sir Henry, and Zelina waited in her cabin as she had been told to do.

Her bags were packed and she was wearing a travelling-cape which was extremely pretty, lined and bordered with fur.

Lord Charnock had told her that it could be very chilly in the Baltic when the winds were coming from the North, and it was wise to take no chances.

At the same time, she knew she felt cold because she was frightened.

Supposing those who were meeting Lord Charnock refused to take her on the Royal Yacht? Then she would have to go on alone, and now she felt frantically that if she lost the man she thought of as her guide and protector, it would be even worse than if she had not met him in the first place.

'It has made me aware how ignorant I am about everything except the things I have read about in books,' she thought miserably. 'I had not realised before that real life is very, very different.'

After what seemed to her hours, she was told that there was a carriage waiting for her on the Quayside.

She jumped up eagerly, in such a hurry to leave the ship that she remembered only with an effort that she should thank the stewardess for her kindness and tip her generously, and also that she must say good-bye and thank the Purser.

She was surprised to find the Captain waiting for her at the top of the gangplank, and when he wished her *"Bon Voyage"* and told her to take care of herself in Russia, she felt suddenly afraid that she was leaving behind for a very long time everything that was England.

Then she remembered that she still had three days left with Lord Charnock, and she hurried down the gangplank to the carriage to find that her luggage was already being piled on top of it.

She had only to travel a short distance to another part of the harbour to board the *Ischora*.

It was a very large and elegant-looking vessel, and once she had been welcomed aboard by Sir Henry and General Suchtelen, Zelina was extremely impressed by her new surroundings.

The General told her that the ship was a fast sailer, manned by a crew of sixty, and Zelina realised its importance when, as the ship weighed anchor, salutes were fired from all the batteries on shore and answered by the *Ischora*.

She did not see Lord Charnock until they met at luncheon, and by that time Zelina had been astonished and delighted by her cabin.

Like all the other cabins in the ship, she learnt later, it was fitted out in satins and the walls were of coloured woods which were very beautiful.

When Sir Henry told her he had managed at a moment's notice to provide her with a lady's-maid as far as St. Petersburg, she also was aware how eloquently Lord Charnock must have described her social position.

"I am afraid my wife is rather annoyed with me for depleting our household, Miss Tiverton," he said, "but it is important that you should have a woman with you, not only to wait on you but to help preserve the

Introducing the Romantic World of Barbara Cartland Fragrances

A world of rare and exotic perfumes…
Inspired by the intensely romantic raptures
of love in every Barbara Cartland novel.

Experience the World of Barbara Cartland Fragrances

Awaken the romantic in your soul. With the mysteriously beautiful perfumes of romance inspired by Barbara Cartland. There's a heady floral bouquet called *The Heart Triumphant,* an exotic Oriental essence named *Moments of Love* and *Love Wins,* a tantalizing woodsy floral. Each of the three, blended with the poetry and promise of love. For every woman who has ever yearned to love. Yesterday, today and especially tomorrow!

Available at fragrance counters everywhere.

Helena Rubinstein®

proprieties when you are travelling in a ship in which otherwise there are only men."

"Please, will you thank your wife so very, very sincerely?" Zelina said.

"Lord Charnock has told me of your unselfishness in leaving your own maid in England," Sir Henry went on, "but I am sure Davey, who is a very experienced woman, will do her best to see to your comfort."

"It is so kind of you," Zelina murmured, feeling guilty when he spoke of her "unselfishness."

Davey was a woman nearing fifty with grey hair who looked like a rather formidable English Nanny.

She was, Zelina thought, exactly the type of lady's-maid with whom a young girl should travel abroad, and she knew that her mother would have approved and she was sure Lord Charnock would also.

The conversation at luncheon was interesting but of course completely impersonal.

Besides the General there was a Doctor who was apparently resident aboard the Royal Yacht, and there was also a Librarian who was returning to St. Petersburg from Europe where he had been purchasing books on behalf of his Imperial Master.

Zelina talked to him eagerly and found that he spoke a great number of languages and was so fluent in English that it was hard to believe he was in fact a pure-bred Russian.

When the meal was over, Lord Charnock said to Zelina:

"I want you to come on deck and have a last glimpse of Denmark. You will find the view of it from here beautiful, and I am only sorry you could not see more of that delightful country."

Zelina followed him onto the deck, and as they stood looking back at the land they had left behind, he said in a low voice:

"There is something I forgot to tell you."

"What is it?" Zelina asked.

"Whatever you say in Russia is always likely to be listened to, noted, and recorded."

Zelina looked startled before she said:

"Are you speaking of the . . . Secret Police, of whom I have heard? But I am of no importance."

"Everybody who is foreign is of importance to the members of that organisation," Lord Charnock said. "That is why you should not mention them by name."

"You do not . . . think they might be . . . interested in me?"

"Of course it also depends to whom you are speaking."

"It must be very . . . difficult for . . . somebody like . . . you."

"It is difficult for everybody who visits Russia, and that is why I am warning you. Think before you speak on any subject which is in the least controversial, and never, never criticise the powers-that-be!"

She was aware that he was referring to the Tsar, and she said quickly:

"I will be careful . . . and thank you for . . . warning me."

Almost as if he thought they might be overheard even though they were on deck, Lord Charnock pointed to the coast they were leaving and said to Zelina:

"I wish from here you could see the Castle of Drottingholm—a curious old building."

"You have travelled to so many places," Zelina said. "I forgot to ask you if you have ever been to Russia before."

"Not in an official capacity," Lord Charnock replied. "But as a young man I stayed in St. Petersburg with some relatives of the Tsar soon after he came to the throne, and twice I have stayed with Russian friends on their Estates in other parts of the country."

"I wish you had time to tell me about them," Zelina remarked.

"I am sure you will find that the Librarian is willing to give you a verbally guided tour of every famous building in Russia!" Lord Charnock replied.

Zelina knew he was joking. At the same time, she thought he had no wish to tell her about his own experiences in Russia and that once again he was rebuking her for being too curious.

The Librarian was only too pleased to offer her quite a number of books to read on the voyage, and she found that after those first few moments with Lord Charnock on deck she was never again alone with him.

The weather became fine and calm, and after they had sailed with considerable speed up the Baltic they sailed past the entrance to the Gulf of Bothnia and the Island of Aland, and anchored at the entrance to the Gulf of Finland.

Zelina found that when it was dark the ship usually anchored, then set off again at first light.

It was Davey the maid who told Zelina, when from the port-hole she could see the towers of Tallin, that they were now exactly twenty-four hours from St. Petersburg.

The Northern Lights appeared and after dinner they went on deck where the Russian crew danced and sang for them.

It was something which Zelina gathered was always done for distinguished visitors. She thought Lord Charnock looked rather bored, but to her it was exciting in a manner that was very hard to describe.

The dancing was graceful, notwithstanding that it had at times a grotesque savagery which was almost violent.

Yet the music, which Zelina was certain was the same as that played by the Russian gypsies, moved her in a way which she had not expected.

She had always wanted to see the dancing and hear the singing of gypsies, and the violins seemed to play on her heart.

As she sat forward in her chair, her eyes fixed on the man dancing wildly in front of them, she had no idea that Lord Charnock was watching her.

She was aware only that the music was arousing feelings that she had never known existed, and for Lord Charnock, whatever he had thought before, it redoubled his conviction that it was wrong for anybody so young and inexperienced to be left alone amongst a people whose emotions were often uncontrollable.

He could see the breath coming quickly between Zelina's parted lips and he knew from his vast experience of women that her heart was beating excitedly in her breast and that feelings she did not understand were rising inside her almost like a flame.

'That child should go back to England on the first ship!' he thought, but knew he could do nothing about it.

When the dancing and singing were finished and Zelina had clapped her hands until they were sore, she said excitedly:

"That was wonderful! An experience I never expected!"

"You will get used to it," Lord Charnock said in a bored voice. "The Russians sing interminably of their sorrows, because they have few joys, just as they dance to forget."

She knew he was trying to dampen down her enthusiasm, and she smiled at him as she said:

"To me it is new, and it was with the greatest difficulty that I did not get up and dance too."

Lord Charnock thought that if she had done so she would have performed with a grace that the Russians, who loved the Ballet, would undoubtedly have appreciated, but he merely said somewhat crushingly:

"You should not attempt to compete with those who have danced and sung from the moment they left the cradle."

When she was alone in her cabin after Davey had left her, Zelina found herself still throbbing with the feelings that the music and the dancing had evoked.

'If that were all there is to Russia, I would love it!' she thought.

Then she remembered what she had read of the cruelties that had been perpetrated in Poland, and she felt herself shiver.

All the same, for the first time since she had left England she had no wish to return—not, at any rate, until she had seen and listened to a great deal more that was Russian.

Chapter Four

Lord Charnock, looking round the impressive Drawing-Room of the British Embassy, thought with a feeling of satisfaction that he had been very clever.

He was well aware that when the Earl of Durham's invitation to Prince Ivan and Princess Olga Volkonsky included Zelina, it set the seal on the impression that she had managed to convey, which was that she had come to Russia solely as a guest, not as an employee.

Hibbert, who always acted as a spy for his Master, had discovered from the other servants that Zelina was having meals with her host and hostess and they had already introduced her to the Royal Family.

Lord Charnock deliberately kept out of Zelina's way and even contrived not to attend certain functions at which he knew she would be present.

He was well aware that if it was thought that he was in any way interested in her, the fact that she had travelled with him would be the subject of gossip amongst the chattering tongues of St. Petersburg, always ready to assume the "worst" of every woman, especially if she was outstandingly pretty.

Watching Zelina dancing with one of the Tsar's attachés, he thought that it would be impossible for any English girl to look more like a traditional English rose.

The waltz, which was originally a German country-dance, had been introduced to England in 1812 by the Princess de Lieven, the wife of the Russian Ambassador.

But nobody had ventured to dance it at Almack's, the most exclusive Club in London, until Tsar Alexander, on his visit to England in 1816, danced it there.

After that, England as well as the rest of Europe adopted the waltz whole-heartedly, and in Russia it had particularly caught the fancy of the young Princes.

The fact that a man could seize his partner round the waist and clasp her to him in public was not only sensational but made flirtations very much easier.

Lord Charnock noted with approval that Zelina was keeping a respectable distance from her partner, although he was talking to her intimately and looking at her with an expression in his eyes which brought a frown to His Lordship's forehead.

"The girl is really too young for this sort of thing," he told himself.

At the same time, he knew that her position, although she was not aware of it, would have been very much more precarious if she had been classed as nothing but a Governess to the Princess's children.

Because he was perceptive he had guessed how apprehensive Zelina was feeling when she bade him a conventional good-bye after the Royal Yacht had arrived in St. Petersburg.

There were a number of important officials to meet Lord Charnock, and he deliberately left it to General Suchtelen to introduce Zelina and explain why she was on board the *Ischora*.

Only when he was alone with the Earl of Durham did he say what a nuisance it had been to find on the English ship a young girl who was in the predicament of being unchaperoned and without even a lady's-maid in attendance.

He added that it was impossible to allow her to travel on to Stockholm, adding:

"Sir Henry Watkin Williams-Winn was horrified at the idea!"

"There was nothing you could do," the Earl of Durham said, "except bring her with you on the *Ischora*."

"I think you might drop a hint to the Russian Ambassador in London that the arrangement anyway had been badly planned and was not what one would expect for the niece of the Earl and Countess of Rothbury."

"I shall certainly do that," the Earl replied, "but you know as well as I do that if the Russians can muddle things, they always do."

Lord Charnock was quite sure that the Earl would enjoy asserting his authority in the matter.

It was known that his ability, sincerity, and charm were marred by a great personal vanity and a susceptibility to flattery. Although he was an extremely intelligent man, this was obviously his Achilles' heel.

The British Embassy carriages had conveyed Zelina, with Davey as a companion, to the Volkonsky Palace.

It had been arranged that the maid would stay with her for a few days, then travel back to Copenhagen on the first available ship leaving St. Petersburg.

Zelina was very glad to have her because she felt that Davey was a support and a comfort in the part she had to play. She knew this would be more difficult to carry out than anything she had ever done before.

Nevertheless, a pride that she had not known she possessed made her raise her chin high.

As she stepped out at the Volkonsky Palace and gave her name to a resplendent Major-Domo, she was aware that he noticed she had arrived in a carriage which bore the British coat-of-arms.

He also glanced at Davey with what she thought was an expression of surprise, then said in somewhat broken French:

"Their Highnesses will I think receive you, *M'mselle*, before you are shown upstairs."

Zelina merely inclined her head as an acknowl-
edgement; then, holding herself very tall and moving
deliberately slowly, she followed the Major-Domo.

They crossed a resplendent Hall with pillars of
malachite and climbed an enormous golden and crystal
staircase to what she was to learn later was one of the
smaller Salons.

However, it seemed at this moment very large,
and it was hung with some magnificent paintings by the
great Masters.

There were flowers everywhere that scented the
room, and at the far end, seated on a sofa with a
Russian wolfhound at his feet, was an extremely good-
looking man whom she identified as her host.

Standing talking to him was a woman who might
easily have stepped from one of the paintings on the
walls.

The Princess Olga, with her huge dark eyes and
her dark hair drawn back from an oval forehead, was a
Western European's ideal of a Russian beauty.

"*M'mselle* Zelina Tiverton!" the Major-Domo announced, and Zelina saw the surprise in the eyes of the
Prince and Princess as she advanced towards them.

She had dressed herself with the greatest care,
making Davey have one of her trunks brought up from
the bowels of the ship and taking from it a very elegant
gown which her aunt had bought her as an afternoon
ensemble.

Zelina had expected to wear it at one of the
Receptions to which she knew her aunt was invited,
such as those given by the great Whig hostesses who
entertained those who supported the Government in
power.

However, she had been left at home by her aunt,
and now she thought it was certainly not the gown that
would be worn by a Governess, nor was the bonnet,

with its small pink feathers and frill of real lace attached to the high crown, one likely to be seen in any School-Room.

She advanced without hurrying down the long Salon until at exactly the correct distance from the Princess she dropped a very graceful curtsey.

Then with a smile she exclaimed eagerly:

"I have arrived earlier than you expected, Your Highness, owing to a series of misadventures, but I am so delighted to be here and it is so very, very kind of you to invite me to stay."

"We are surprised to see you, Miss Tiverton," the Princess replied in perfect English.

The Prince, who had risen, held out his hand, and as Zelina curtseyed again he said:

"Welcome to Russia! I am sorry to hear that your journey has been an uncomfortable one."

"Not exactly uncomfortable, Your Highness," Zelina replied. "In fact, the *Ischora* is the most beautiful ship I have ever seen!"

"The *Ischora!*" the Princess exclaimed.

Zelina laughed, and it sounded quite natural.

"That is why I have arrived earlier than expected, and I must tell Your Highness that as my Chaperone was ill and had to be left behind, my lady's-maid is not my own, but borrowed from Lady Watkin Williams-Winn in Copenhagen."

By the time she had assuaged the Prince and Princess's curiosity and explained the commotion which had been caused by her Chaperone's illness, Zelina knew they had both accepted that she was a guest in their Palace, and they had not even mentioned their children.

It was only at luncheon when a number of guests appeared that Zelina realised she made the numbers odd.

Because she was present, there was one woman

too many, and she knew that it was only Lord Charnock's cleverness which had prevented her from being dismissed to the School-Room to eat with the children and their other attendants.

Much later in the day, when the children appeared to spend an hour with their mother before the youngest of them went to bed, Zelina found that there were five, starting at the age of three and ending with an attractive girl of fourteen.

They had an English Nanny, a French *Mademoiselle*, and a Music Teacher, and the boys had visiting Tutors in Greek and Latin, besides two Riding-masters.

"Your children are very well educated," she said to the Princess.

"I hope they will be," was the reply, "but I am rather worried that they may not speak English correctly."

"I thought their English very good."

"They have of course learnt it from their Nurse," the Princess explained, "but I am well aware that, excellent woman though she is, she is hardly what you would call a cultured person."

There was a pause, and Zelina knew that the Princess was waiting for her to say she would teach the children to speak English.

Remembering Lord Charnock's advice, she merely said:

"I am sure that as they talk with you, Your Highness, and that as your English is perfect, they will not make any mistakes that could not be easily rectified."

She saw that a suggestion trembled on the Princess's lips, but before she could speak Zelina added:

"Oh, I wish my father could have seen the treasures you have in this wonderful Palace! When he was a soldier he appreciated Art, and it is because we were so close that I have a little knowledge of painting, which will certainly be increased while I am in Russia."

"Your father was in the Army?" the Princess asked.

It was easy from that opening to introduce her grandfather and to speak of some of the paintings that were owned by her uncle the Earl of Rothbury.

Like Lord Charnock, she was aware that when the invitation arrived from the British Embassy for dinner and a dance, it finally swept away from the Prince and Princess's mind any idea that they might use her as a teacher for their children.

When she had come down to luncheon she had presented the Princess with a gift, which Lord Charnock had told her was an important thing to do.

She had found three fans in the trunk which Davey had unpacked, all of them in white satin boxes which bore the name of the well-known shop in Bond Street in which her aunt had purchased them.

Because they were so pretty, she really wished to keep them for herself, but Zelina had chosen for the Princess the one she liked the least, and even then, because she had owned so few extravagant things in her life, it was quite hard to part with it.

Davey, however, had wrapped it up very elegantly in paper and tied it with a piece of satin ribbon which belonged to one of Zelina's gowns.

The Princess had been delighted.

"How very, very kind of you, Miss Tiverton!" she had exclaimed.

Then as she looked at the fan with a little smile she had added:

"I cannot speak to you in such a formal manner. 'Zelina' is a very attractive and very Russian name, although you will never look anything but English."

The gentleman who was seated next to her at luncheon had said much the same thing.

"I know you come from England, where there are so many beautiful women," he had said. "Now tell me about yourself."

Again Zelina remembered that she must impress

the Russians, and when several of the Princess's guests said they hoped they would meet her again, she knew she had been successful.

When she went upstairs to dress for dinner, Davey told her that because they had arrived unexpectedly, the Princess had sent a groom to invite another gentleman to dine.

"You've caused quite a sensation, Miss, arriving in the Royal Yacht," she said, "and, from what I learnt downstairs, nearly a week early!"

"I am so glad I did not have to go on to Stockholm and travel from there in a Russian ship," Zelina said.

As she spoke she thought how frightening it had been, then added:

"And I am very lucky to have had you to look after me. Which gown shall I wear this evening?"

This took a little time to decide, because Zelina had always been certain that first impressions were important, apart from the fact that she was still, on Lord Charnock's instructions, establishing herself.

When she was dressed she longed to tell him how well his plans had worked and that after tonight there would be no doubt what her position in the Palace was.

Because of his warning to her aboard the *Ischora*, and because she guessed that if the Russians listened to what was said, they would certainly also read what was written, she did not write to thank him as she longed to do.

"He will guess how grateful I am," she told herself.

At the same time, she thought that she was being very remiss in not making it clear to him.

'One day I hope I will be able to say so,' she thought.

Wearing one of her prettiest gowns from Bond Street and knowing that she would not be overshadowed by the Russians who bought their gowns in Paris, she went down the gold and crystal staircase to the Salon where the Princess was receiving her guests before dinner.

The following evening, because she was certain that she would see Lord Charnock at the British Embassy, Zelina had decided to wear the loveliest gown she owned.

She had anticipated when her aunt had bought it that it would be a gown she could wear only if she were invited to a Ball at Buckingham Palace.

Now as she dressed she thought that she would rather impress Lord Charnock than Queen Adelaide, although she was afraid it was unlikely that he would take any notice of her.

She had not missed what the Princess had said about him to the other ladies who had come to luncheon the previous day.

"I suppose you are going to the British Embassy tomorrow evening?" one of them had remarked.

"Yes, of course," the Princess replied.

"I expect Lord Charnock will be a guest of the Ambassador, even though he is staying at the Palace with His Imperial Majesty."

"Of course Lord Charnock will be there!" the Prince said. "And I look forward to renewing my acquaintance with him. The last time I saw him was in Paris."

The lady to whom he was speaking laughed.

"Where he is very much *engagé*. I hear that all the attractive women there pursued him, but he was attached irrevocably to the exquisite Sophie."

"Sophie would certainly not allow him to be anything else!" the Princess remarked, and they laughed.

"I believe, however, that it is all over," another woman joined in, "but then His Lordship's *affaires de coeur* never last long and are so discreet that, as somebody once suggested, they are almost nonexistent."

"That is not the story I have been told," the

Princess said. "And those quiet, silent, self-controlled Englishmen are often extremely ardent lovers."

"You should know, dearest," one lady said almost spitefully.

But the Princess adroitly turned the conversation to another subject.

Zelina was astonished at what she had heard.

She had never thought of Lord Charnock as a man who might be an ardent lover, and it struck her that he must in consequence have found her very boring and inexperienced.

Then she was certain that the Princess and her friends were mistaken, for he was far too involved with his work to have time for anything else.

Nevertheless, when she saw him across the room at the British Embassy, she found herself wondering if he was enamoured with the very beautiful woman to whom he was speaking.

Zelina would have been incredulous if she had been told that the lady in question had been recruited by the Secret Police with the full approval of the Tsar.

In fact, her instructions were to find out why Lord Charnock had come to St. Petersburg and as much as possible about the English Foreign Secretary's attitude towards Russia.

There was a certain secret which the Tsar was extremely anxious to conceal from the British, and although he did not believe they had any suspicions of it, he had ordered a thorough investigation of Lord Charnock.

Because the Tsar believed so firmly in his ability not only to get his own way in everything he undertook but also to deceive and hoodwink his opponents, he was not aware that in Lord Charnock he had met his match.

On his guard from the moment he had stepped on board the *Ischora*, Lord Charnock had been aware that General Suchtelen, while apparently talking in the

most open manner about anything and everything, was
making a note of his answers which would eventually be
repeated to the Tsar.

He was equally aware when he had first been
introduced to the Countess Natasha Obolensky that she
had been chosen to seduce him into every possible
indiscretion.

She was very lovely, with eyes that slanted up-
wards at the corners and a face that might have been
moulded by a master craftsman in mediaeval times.

Everything she said seemed to have a slight chal-
lenge, and every movement of her lips was a provoca-
tive invitation to the man to whom she was speaking.

She flirted with Lord Charnock outrageously, at
the same time being clever enough to appear slightly
elusive.

They sparred verbally with each other at dinner,
and when the Tsar singled him out for an intimate talk,
Lord Charnock noticed that the Countess made no
attempt to attach herself to anybody else, but merely
waited for him to be free.

The first night that Lord Charnock stayed at the
Imperial Palace he slept peacefully and undisturbed.

He had been amused when he went up to his
extremely impressive bedroom to find that Hibbert had
been taking the usual precautions that they always
carried out in every country he visited.

The valet had not said anything but had merely
tapped one of the panels, which immediately opened
with a secret spring.

Lord Charnock saw that behind the panel the wall
was hollow and knew that anybody occupying the ad-
joining room would be able to hear everything that was
said in his bedroom.

This was something which they had encountered
before, and Lord Charnock saw that his valet had taken

the goose-feather mattress from the bed, which his Master disliked, and squeezed it into the aperture.

Now it would not only be impossible for anybody to enter it, but no-one could overhear what was being said.

Hibbert indicated that as far as he could discover the rest of the room was clear, but he pointed up at the painted ceiling and Lord Charnock saw there was a piece of paper stuck over the eye of a goddess.

He knew this indicated that Hibbert had found a peep-hole through it from the floor above.

He said nothing, but merely smiled at Hibbert to congratulate him, and while he undressed they talked only when it was necessary.

He took his bath and dressed again in his evening-clothes.

In his silk knee-breeches and wearing his numerous decorations pinned to his evening-coat, with a white cravat which would rival that of any Dandy of the Russian Court, Lord Charnock looked very impressive as he walked the long distance to the Tsar's apartments where he was to dine.

The food was excellent, the wines superlative, and the conversation intelligent and stimulating.

It was the sort of evening which Lord Charnock enjoyed, when the guests talked instead of being obliged to dance and the Tsar and Tsarina retired early.

Somebody suggested he might wish to go on to a Ball, but he declined, saying that he was tired after his journey, and he was then able to escape to his own room.

Hibbert was waiting for him, and again without saying anything aloud he pointed to the despatch-cases, which told Lord Charnock that they had been slightly moved from the position in which they had been left.

Another gesture from Hibbert indicated that his

possessions had all been inspected, the drawers opened, and anything in writing had been read.

Since this was what he had expected would happen, Lord Charnock was not in the least disturbed, and when he got into bed he slept dreamlessly until the morning.

He awoke ready to face the day, knowing that he had to consider every word he spoke and to control even the expression in his eyes in case it should give away what he was thinking.

He was not surprised to find that the Countess Natasha was seated next to him at luncheon and again at dinner.

The party on the second night was very different from the first and very much larger.

The women were ablaze with jewels, and when dinner was over more guests arrived from other Palaces and they danced in one of the magnificent Ball-Rooms with its gold pillars symbolic of the glittering extravagance of everything and everybody in Imperial Russia.

Lord Charnock was not particularly eager to dance, but he could not refuse the Countess when she asked him to do so, and he was aware that the Tsar seemed to smile at them with approval as they moved past him.

"You are so handsome, *mon cher!*" the Countess said in a voice that seemed to vibrate with feeling.

"Thank you," Lord Charnock replied, "and as you are well aware that you are very beautiful, there is no point in my telling you so."

"But I want you to say so, and I want to feel that it is not just an expression which comes from your lips but from your heart."

"I have always been told that is an organ which has been omitted from my anatomy," Lord Charnock said dryly.

"That I am sure is untrue, and you must let me find it for you, which will be very exciting for me."

"But perhaps a discomfort where I am concerned."

"I think actually it would make you very happy. Shall we try to find your heart?"

Because Lord Charnock could not think of an answer to the question, he smiled enigmatically but did not reply, and he felt her press herself a little closer to him.

It was late when the party finished and later still when Lord Charnock was ready for bed.

He did not, however, get into the large, heavily draped bed with its lace-edged silk sheets monogrammed with the Royal cipher, but stood at the window looking out at the lights on buildings across the Neva and seeing the stars overhead reflected in the water moving slowly towards the sea.

He was wondering whether Hibbert had successfully blocked every secret entrance to the bedroom when he had filled in the gap between the two walls.

It was then that another panel in a wall, which obviously Hibbert had not discovered, slid open and Natasha appeared.

She was looking exceedingly lovely and very seductive in a diaphanous robe which matched her eyes and was clasped at the neck with a very large emerald.

She shut the panel behind her and she and Lord Charnock were looking at each other.

It flashed through his mind that if he sent her away it would cause consternation amongst the Secret Police, and he knew it would also severely damage Natasha's reputation as being the most experienced seductress in the Russian Court.

Then with a little movement as sinuous as that of a serpent she moved towards him and her arms went round his neck.

"You did not say good-night to me properly," she said, lifting her lips to his.

Just for a moment Lord Charnock hesitated, then

he thought cynically that it was all part of the game and
it would be a pity if he showed too quickly that he did
not underestimate his opponent.

Then as he kissed her and felt the fire on her lips,
he knew that at least that was spontaneous and had not
been ignited to order by the Secret Police or anybody
else.

*   *   *

Now in the British Embassy, as Natasha commanded
his attention by right, Lord Charnock was at the same
time acutely aware of Zelina.

There was no need for her to tell him that she had
been successful in assuming her rightful position in the
household where she was staying.

The mere fact that she was present tonight and
dressed in a gown which only a débutante would wear
told him what had happened without words.

Then as the evening progressed Lord Charnock
knew, with a perception which sometimes worked whether he wished it to do so or not, that Zelina was longing
and yearning for him to dance with her.

At first he resisted what was almost a cry from her
heart to his.

Then he told himself that any man in his position
would give a woman of the same nationality the courte-
sy of enquiring after her well-being, considering that
she was alone in a strange land.

Accordingly, when Zelina had almost given up
hope, he walked across to where she was sitting by the
Princess to say:

"There is no need to ask if you are enjoying
yourself. I can see that your hostess is being very
hospitable, as might be expected from anybody so gra-
cious and so charming."

As he spoke, he raised the Princess's hand to his
lips and said:

"Thank you for being kind to one of my compatriots."

"I have heard of the difficulties which the poor child had in reaching here," the Princess answered.

"It certainly was a chapter of disasters, but Sir Henry Watkin Williams-Winn proved to be a Fairy-Godfather," Lord Charnock answered lightly, "and provided not only a Royal vessel in which Miss Tiverton could travel, but also a lady's-maid."

"I have always found Sir Henry a magical man, and you too, My Lord," the Princess said.

"You flatter me!" Lord Charnock replied.

Somebody else came up to speak to the Princess and he turned to Zelina.

"May I have the pleasure of this dance?" he asked. "I am afraid you will find me not as light of foot as the Russians who entertained us aboard the *Ischora*."

"I would love to dance with you!" Zelina said simply.

She rose as she spoke, and he knew by the light in her eyes that it was something she wanted very much.

They moved round the floor to the romantic music of a dozen violins, and when they were out of hearing of the Princess, Zelina said in a low voice:

"You were so clever! Everything went exactly as you planned it."

"I am glad," Lord Charnock replied.

"I wanted so much to write and tell you how grateful I am, but I thought it would be a mistake."

"Definitely a mistake!" he agreed.

"I can only now say thank you, thank you!" Zelina said. "I wish there were more adequate words in which I could express myself."

"I am delighted that everything has worked out so well for you," Lord Charnock said, "and now enjoy yourself."

"Everybody has been very kind, and I am trying

not to think of the things which . . . shocked me before I . . . came here."

"That is sensible."

They danced for a little while in silence. Then Zelina said:

"You will not leave without telling me . . . without saying . . . good-bye?"

"I am not thinking of leaving for a while," Lord Charnock replied.

He saw by the expression on her face that this was what she had hoped to hear, and her eyes were very revealing as she said:

"I may not see you, but it is so . . . comforting to know you are . . . here in the same city . . . and that if anything . . . awful should happen I could . . . find you."

"Nothing 'awful' will happen," Lord Charnock said firmly, "and you must stop being afraid. Just remember that most girls of your age think only of enjoying themselves, and start each day with that intention."

"I will . . . try," Zelina said, "and I will remember . . . everything you have told me."

"Then nothing will upset you."

As he spoke the dance came to an end, and as he turned to walk back with Zelina across the floor to the Princess, a voice beside him said:

"Good-evening, My Lord! Delightful to see you again!"

Lord Charnock turned to see Prince Alexis Stoganoff holding out his hand.

The Prince was a man he had met frequently in Paris and once or twice in London, but he was someone for whom he had no great liking.

The Prince, immensely wealthy and of great importance at Court, had been described as a Don Juan, a

Casanova, and more simply as a Russian with a charm that no woman could resist.

Lord Charnock was also aware that his affairs of the heart were often unsavoury and in some cases reprehensible.

"I heard you had arrived," Prince Alexis said now, "and also that you had brought with you such a beautiful English rose that our Russian orchids have turned green with envy!"

As he spoke he was looking at Zelina, and, ignoring Lord Charnock's quick assertion that he had not personally brought her to Russia with him, said:

"Please present me. It is impossible for me to wait any longer to meet so lovely a flower."

There was nothing Lord Charnock could do but say:

"Miss Zelina Tiverton—His Highness Prince Alexis Stoganoff!"

Zelina curtseyed and the Prince reached out and took her hand in both of his.

"I cannot believe that you have not stepped right out of my dreams," he said in a deep voice, "except that if you are real, I shall never be able to dream again, realising how completely inadequate my imagination has been!"

Zelina gave a little laugh, and the Prince asked:

"Why are you laughing at me?"

"Because you sound exactly like somebody in a book," she replied. "I never thought human beings really spoke that way!"

Lord Charnock thought with satisfaction that Zelina's reply was certainly something the Prince was not in the habit of hearing, but he said:

"If you are cruel to me, you will throw me into a despondency which will be desperately hard to combat."

Again Zelina gave a little laugh.

"The Princess has told me," she said, "that the Tsar's favourite reading is Sir Walter Scott, but Your Highness is even more dramatic than Ivanhoe!"

"You are enchanting!" the Prince exclaimed.

He raised Zelina's hand to his lips and kissed it.

"I think," Lord Charnock intervened, "I should take you back to Her Highness."

"Do not leave me!" the Prince cried. "If you will dance with me it will lift me into the Seventh Heaven."

"Perhaps later, Your Highness," Zelina replied. "I think now . . . as His Lordship suggests, I should return to Her Highness."

She curtseyed and moved away before the Prince could protest further.

She knew without being told that Lord Charnock was pleased with her behaviour.

As they walked towards the Princess he said in a low voice:

"Beware of that man! Have nothing to do with him!"

Zelina nodded, and then when they reached the Princess, Lord Charnock said:

"I am returning Zelina to you, and she has told me what an enjoyable time she is having. I am sure her uncle and aunt will be extremely grateful for Your Highness's kindness."

"It is a pleasure to have somebody so young and enthusiastic in the house," the Princess said. "I hope, My Lord, you will find time to dine with us in the next few days?"

"I shall be delighted!" Lord Charnock replied.

He bowed politely to the Princess and did not look at Zelina before he walked away.

As he did so, she thought that there was nobody in the whole room to equal him, and she wished that their dance together was not over but only just beginning.

'I would rather dance with him than anybody else I have ever met,' she thought.

Then as she watched she saw the beautiful woman to whom he had been talking when she had first arrived go to his side and put her hand familiarly on his arm.

Zelina felt a strange feeling that she did not recognise as jealousy.

"What can that Russian woman mean to him?" she wondered. "And who is she?"

Because she was too shy to ask the Princess, she waited until she was dancing with a young man who had sat next to her at dinner.

Then she asked:

"Who is the beautiful lady talking to Lord Charnock?"

Her partner followed the direction of her eyes and replied:

"That is the Countess Natasha Obolensky."

"She is very lovely!"

"A great many men think so," Zelina's partner answered. "She is supposed to have broken more hearts than any other woman in the world!"

"Broken . . . more . . . hearts?" Zelina found it difficult to repeat the words.

"Yes indeed. Two men have committed suicide because of her, and nobody can count the number of duels that have been fought in her honour!"

"She is . . . unmarried?"

Zelina found it difficult to ask the question.

Her partner laughed.

"No. Indeed, she is married to a very distinguished Statesman, but he is at the moment in the South."

It was strange, Zelina thought, but when he had said the Countess was married her heart gave a decided leap and the lights in the room seemed to flare up to the ceiling.

At the same time, as she watched Lord Charnock walking away from the Ball-Room with the Countess on his arm, she felt as if he had left her far behind and once again she was lonely and lost.

Chapter Five

Zelina started when a servant's voice announced:
"His Highness Prince Alexis Stoganoff!"

With a feeling of apprehension she realised that she was alone since the Princess had left the house for a private visit to the Tsarina.

"I cannot ask you to come with me, Zelina," she had said, "as Her Imperial Majesty wishes to see me alone."

"I shall be quite happy," Zelina had answered. "I seldom have time to read the fascinating books which are in your Library, and there is one particular one I am anxious to finish. It is all about St. Petersburg."

The Princess had laughed.

"Then it will certainly take you more than the short time I will be away. There is the Reception this evening at the Michaelov Palace, and I know the Grand Duchess Hélèna is longing to meet you."

"It sounds very exciting!" Zelina had said.

When the Princess had gone she picked up the book of which she had read about half.

Seating herself comfortably in the window of the Salon d'Or, which was where they sat when they were alone, she soon forgot everything but what she was reading.

Now she rose to her feet, aware that the one thing she did not want was to be alone with Prince Alexis.

Ever since Lord Charnock had introduced him to

her at the British Embassy, he had pursued her with a determination which she found frightening.

She did not like the expression in his eyes, she mistrusted the flattery which came so easily to his lips, and when she was obliged to dance with him she knew he held her too closely, and he was quite impervious to snubs.

Now as he reached her side he lifted her hand to his lips, and his kiss was by no means a polite gesture but was passionate and insistent.

"I am afraid, Your Highness," Zelina said, "I am alone, and the servants should have informed you of the fact."

"They did!" the Prince replied. "But as the Princess is not here, I can talk to you as I have been wanting to do ever since I first saw you."

"You are well aware that to do so is . . . incorrect," Zelina said in what she hoped was a cold voice but which actually sounded very young and unsure.

"When you know me better, which I intend you shall," the Prince replied, "you will learn that I never do what is correct, but what I want to do, which is a very different thing."

"Then if you . . . will not . . . leave me," Zelina said, "I must leave . . . you."

She did not look at him as she spoke.

She tried to speak in a dignified, calm manner, but she was aware that her heart was fluttering like a frightened bird in her breast, and if she obeyed her impulse she would have run away as quickly as she could.

Everything she had heard about the Prince, everything he had said to her when they had danced together, and the way he looked at her, had frightened her almost unbearably.

She told herself that she was being foolish and it would be impossible for him to hurt her when she was a guest of the Prince and Princess.

At the same time, she had been in St. Petersburg long enough to learn that everybody seemed to be involved in love-affairs of some sort, and she was certain that already the Prince's attentions to her had not gone unnoticed.

"Do you really think I would allow you to leave me?"

He spoke lightly, but there was a note in his voice which told Zelina that if she tried to go he would certainly prevent her from doing so, which would involve his touching her physically.

In fear of this, she hesitated. Then she said:

"If you really have something you wish to talk to me about . . . then I will listen . . . but please . . . Your Highness, make it short. If the Princess returns and finds you here, she will think it very . . . strange that I am . . . receiving in her . . . . absence."

"I assure you she will think nothing of the sort!" the Prince replied. "She is well versed in love—and love, my beautiful English rose, is what I wish to discuss with you."

Zelina drew herself up stiffly.

"That is . . . something I do not . . . wish to . . . hear."

"Why not? Love concerns every woman, and I have never in my life felt so convinced that I am the right person to teach you about the most alluring, exciting, and tantalising feeling of which the human body is capable."

There was a deep note in his voice now, and as Zelina sat down on the sofa he seated himself beside her, and, to her consternation, he was unpleasantly close.

She managed to move a little farther away from him but now she was against the arm of the sofa.

"I love you, Zelina!" the Prince said. "I love you until I feel it is impossible when I have met you to live through the hours until I shall see you again. What have you done to me that I should feel like this?"

Zelina looked away from him across the room, conscious that there was a tremor in her voice as she replied:

"Please . . . Your Highness . . . you must not . . . say such . . . things to . . . me."

"Why not? And you have to listen to me! I want you, Zelina, and I know I can make you very happy."

He sighed before he went on:

"If I could ask you to marry me, I would, but I expect you are aware that I am married, and it is a very unhappy alliance."

Zelina stiffened at the word "marriage," and now she asked, her voice sounding unexpectedly loud:

"You are . . . married?"

"Yes, of course," the Prince replied. "In Russia our marriages are arranged when we are very young, and my wife was chosen for me by my parents."

"B-but you have . . . a wife!"

"Yes, yes, but she need not concern us."

"She certainly concerns me!" Zelina retorted. "And I think it wrong . . . very wrong of Your Highness to speak to me as you have when you are a . . . married man, and your . . . loyalty should be with the . . . woman who bears your . . . name."

The Prince shrugged his shoulders.

"She does not count any more. We live in separate parts of the country, and I am offering you my heart, Zelina. Surely that means something which could unite us more closely than any wedding-ring?"

Zelina rose to her feet.

"I have no wish to hear Your Highness speak in such a way," she said. "I am shocked that you should speak of your marriage as if it were of no . . . consequence, and it is not a . . . compliment that you should . . . offer me your love . . . but in my opinion an . . . insult!"

She thought the Prince would be abashed, but instead he held her hand in both of his so that she could not escape, and sat looking up at her with a smile on his lips.

"I adore you!" he said. "Could any woman be more fascinating, more alluring, even when she is reprimanding me?"

He kissed her hand, his lips hot and demanding on her skin, and although she tried to free herself she was unable to do so.

"My sweet, adorable little English rose," he said, "I will teach you that nothing is important except love, and love conquers everything."

Zelina tried to pull her hand away from his.

"Please let me go, Your Highness!" she cried. "I have already told you what I feel, and I must ask you as a . . . gentleman to . . . respect my . . . feelings."

The Prince laughed.

"I am not an English gentleman—cold, conventional, and of course very honourable."

He spoke mockingly and went on:

"I am Russian, and a fire burns within me which will light a fire in you. Then you will understand that love is all-consuming, omnipotent, and inescapable!"

He turned over her hand with both of his and pressed his lips passionately on her palm, and although he was only kissing her hand, Zelina felt he was violating her whole body.

"Let me go! Let me go!" she cried.

Then, still holding her captive, the Prince rose to his feet and she knew he was about to put his arms round her.

She gave a little scream of sheer fright, and at that moment, to her utter relief, the door opened and Prince Ivan came into the Salon.

"I did not know you were here, Alexis!" he exclaimed.

His intervention made it possible for Zelina to

release herself from the Prince, and without explanation she ran across the Salon and out through the door.

Prince Ivan raised his eye-brows as he saw her go,
then he looked at the Prince.

"Up to your usual tricks, Alexis?" he enquired.

"She is lovely! Adorable!" the Prince replied. "She
is completely innocent and it will be an inexpressible
fascination to awaken her."

Prince Ivan thought for a moment. Then he said:

"His Majesty does not want any trouble with the
British at this particular moment and in consequence is
making a great fuss of Lord Charnock."

"Surely that does not concern a girl of her age?"
Prince Alexis asked. "Moreover, Natasha will give him
no time to think of any other woman except herself."

"I am sure you are right," Prince Ivan agreed. "At
the same time, the English support each other, and if
this girl should make trouble it would certainly annoy
His Majesty."

Prince Alexis made a very expressive gesture with
his hands.

"I have never known any woman to make a fuss,
except when I leave her."

Prince Ivan laughed.

"Your conceit, Alexis, is abominable, but I admit
you have plenty of grounds for it."

"Leave everything and the lovely Zelina to me,"
Prince Alexis said.

*   *   *

In the security of her bedroom, Zelina thought
how right Lord Charnock had been when he warned
her not to be alone with a Russian.

She decided that the next time the Princess was
out, she would not stay down in one of the Salons but
would lock herself in her own bedroom.

At the same time, because she was frightened, she longed to see Lord Charnock and hear his calm, reassuring voice.

Then she remembered how involved he seemed to be with the Countess Natasha, and she thought with a sinking of her heart that he would have no time for her.

But she could not help thinking of him and in a way yearning for him.

He had been so kind to her on her journey to Russia, and she found herself wishing that they had never arrived but by some strange magic had gone on sailing into the horizon and over the edge of the world into fairy-tale eternity.

*　　*　　*

As it was so unexpected, Zelina could hardly believe it when a day later she found herself in the country, miles from St. Petersburg and staying in one of the most magnificent Palaces she could possibly imagine.

The Princess had come back from her visit to the Tsarina to say that the Tsar wished them to stay with him on his Estate at Tsarskoye Selo and they were to drive there the next morning.

The packing of the trunks and the preparations which galvanised the whole household were something which Zelina had never experienced before and which she found very fascinating.

Davey was not to go with her, as there was a ship leaving for Stockholm in two days' time. However, another lady's-maid from the Princess's household had been found for her and she seemed extremely competent.

She and Davey sorted out the clothes that Zelina would need for Tsarskoye Selo, leaving behind a great number of her other gowns.

"I'll pack them up carefully for you, *Mademoi-*

selle," Davey said, "in case you stay longer than Her Highness expects to do at the moment. Then the rest of your trunks can easily follow you."

"Thank you for being so kind," Zelina replied.

She gave Davey a large tip and also a present of a warm shawl which she had admired when she was unpacking for her.

"It's too much! You mustn't part with it, *Mademoiselle!*" Davey protested.

"I am lucky to have so many things," Zelina replied. "I would like you to have it, and when you wear it think of me.

"I'll do that, *Mademoiselle*," Davey replied, "and I'll always remember you in my prayers."

"Thank you," Zelina said. "I feel I may need them."

She was thinking of Prince Alexis as she spoke, and it was a joy to know that when she was away from St. Petersburg he would not bother her.

However, she was horrified when they assembled for dinner at Tsarskoye Selo, for she found that he too had been invited by the Tsar as a guest.

The fact that he was there would have been more of a shock if Zelina had not learnt with an inexpressible feeling of joy that Lord Charnock was to arrive the following morning.

She naturally had no idea that in fact the party had been arranged because the Tsar was already impatient at the lack of information from the Countess Natasha and the other Agents he had ordered to investigate Lord Charnock.

The Secret Police had even, on their Master's orders, managed in Lord Charnock's absence to pick the locks of two of the despatch-boxes.

Although it was done skilfully and no ordinary Courier or King's Messenger would have been aware that they had been tampered with, Lord Charnock had known it immediately.

However, he had been quite unperturbed, aware not only that the despatch-boxes carried everything in code, which the Russians would find very hard to decipher, but that there was actually little of importance for them to read even if they managed to do so.

The main purpose of his visit, known only to him, was something that was not in writing but was stored in his mind.

He had been amused by the Countess Natasha's efforts to extract information from him when he had been aroused by her fiery love-making, and later, when, as she hoped, he was too relaxed to be on his guard.

Lord Charnock's answers to her questions had proved exceedingly disappointing to the Tsar, and, having berated the Countess and the members of the Secret Police, he decided that he would show up their inefficiency by doing the job himself.

"I want you to see Tsarskoye Selo," he had said to Lord Charnock. "The Empress and I are going there tomorrow, and I hope very much that you will join us."

"I shall be delighted to do so," Lord Charnock had replied, "but I hope Your Majesty will permit me to arrive on the following day, as the British Ambassador has already arranged a dinner-party in my honour tomorrow evening."

The Tsar agreed with a bad grace, and he chose the rest of his house-party carefully, hoping that the inclusion of Zelina and her host and hostess would convince the Englishman that there was no reason to be suspicious as to why he had been invited.

There were also several relatives of the Tsar who he knew would be amusing and witty but were in no way connected with politics.

"I know how to manage these things," the Tsar had

said to the Head of the Secret Police, "and your men are far too stereotyped in their approach to somebody as astute as Lord Charnock."

"I am quite sure Your Imperial Majesty will be successful," Count Benckendorff had replied, thinking as he spoke that it was very unlikely.

Tsarskoye Selo was about two hours' drive from St. Petersburg, and to Zelina it was very exciting to see the countryside as she drove at an almost unbelievable pace in a chariot with four horses abreast.

The Russians she saw by the road-side were fine men, tall and wild-looking. But their high boots, great pelisses of sheepskin, long beards, and tangled hair were all covered with a thick crust of dirt.

Few women were to be seen, but those there were were ugly in form and face.

The Palace was enormous. The Princess had told her it was to be a small and intimate party, but even before Lord Charnock arrived Zelina found that there were over thirty guests.

Dinner was served at five o'clock in an immense *Salle* with a horse-shoe table.

The servants, who were dressed in white turbans and scarlet and gold uniforms, seemed very Eastern.

To Zelina's surprise, her lady's-maid, who although she was Russian could speak quite understandable French, told her that there were four hundred Cooks in the Palace, forty travelled with the Tsar, and every time the Imperial Family went from St. Petersburg to the country four hundred carriages were required.

It was the first time that Zelina had seen the Imperial children, and after dinner two little Grand Dukes came in dressed in Russian costume.

They seemed to be very happy, and when the Tsar made them laugh they rolled about on the floor.

They had their old Scottish Nurse with them and a

French *Mademoiselle*. When the children were dismissed and their attendants went with them, Zelina remembered that had it not been for Lord Charnock's advice, that was what would have happened to her.

After they had finished eating, the Empress dismissed her guests, asking them to return at eight o'clock for a Reception.

Zelina changed her gown again, this time putting on a very elegant Ball-gown. The other ladies in the party were so splendidly gowned that she thought they might have been attending a State Ball.

The Tsarina, who was tall and graceful, wore a dress of white with a necklace of enormous blue sapphires, and even her second daughter, who was only fourteen, was wearing a necklace of perfect pearls and bracelets of diamonds and rubies.

Although the Emperor spoke as if he were living a humble life, it was impossible to imagine that any place could display more eloquently the immense power, wealth, and extravagance of the Royal Court.

After there had been general conversation for two hours, Zelina became aware that Prince Alexis, to whom she had not spoken since she arrived, was edging his way towards her.

Quickly she looked round for the Princess and saw her talking to an elderly woman who was one of the house-party.

She went to her side.

"What is it?" the Princess asked.

"I wonder, Your Highness, if I might retire to bed?" Zelina asked. "I have a slight headache, and although it has been a very exciting day, it has also been a tiring one."

"I think what you are really saying," the Princess replied with a smile, "is that you are exhausted after two Balls at St. Petersburg. As we shall doubtless be late tomorrow night, I think you can slip away. I will make your apologies to Her Imperial Majesty if she notices that you are not here."

"Thank you," Zelina said.

She hurried towards the door, and only when she reached it and looked back did she see an expression of anger on Prince Alexis's face, and she knew she had been wise in eluding him.

The following day she learnt that the Tsar liked everything to be informal when they were in the country, which meant that after he had decided what he would do there was a chance that the rest of the guests would not be given any direct orders.

Lord Charnock arrived early and the Tsar swept him into the garden to admire some improvements he had made and a new fountain surrounded by gods and goddesses encrusted in gold, which had been erected in front of the Palace.

Knowing that Prince Alexis would be watching for her, Zelina kept closely to the Princess's side, and she thought she had been rather clever, until he came up and said to Princess Olga:

"Have I your permission to show our English visitor the Aviary? I am sure she will find the birds collected by Her Imperial Majesty very attractive."

"But of course, Alexis!" the Princess replied. "And if you are thinking of inviting me to come with you, I assure you I have seen them far too many times already!"

Her eyes were twinkling as she spoke, and the Prince replied with a smile:

"I am sorry you will not accompany us, but it would be a pity for Miss Tiverton to miss anything which owes so much to our hostess's artistic skill."

"Of course," the Princess answered, and turned to speak to somebody else.

Zelina longed to refuse to go with the Prince, but as she was wondering how she could do so, the Prince masterfully put his hand under her elbow and drew her along the marble corridors which led to the other end of the Palace.

It was quite a long walk, and as they passed a great number of servants, Zelina did not, despite her apprehension, feel that she was alone with the Prince.

At length they came to the Orangery which had been built on one side of the Palace, and very cleverly constructed at the end of it was the Aviary.

The first part of the building was given over to an indoor garden which Zelina had heard was one of the sights of the Palace. It was where the ladies exercised in the winter when it was impossible to go out-of-doors.

Never had she imagined anything so pretty as orange trees in bloom, creepers climbing up the walls, and flower-boxes on the ground containing every type of flower from orchids to violets, all artificially grown in a way that had been evolved by the Russians through sheer necessity.

The brilliance of the flowers and their fragrance that filled the air made Zelina clap her hands.

"Oh, how lovely! How unbelievably lovely!" she exclaimed.

"And so are you!" the Prince replied.

Immediately she was on her guard, and looked round to find that they were alone and there was not a sign of any servant or attendant.

"Where are the birds?" she asked nervously.

The Prince pointed to where in the distance between the pillars she could see the beginning of the Aviary.

"I will show them to you in a moment, there is no hurry."

"I want to see them," she protested.

"I want you to listen to me."

"There is nothing you can say, Your Highness, that I want to hear."

"I will make you change your mind."

He came a little nearer to her as he spoke.

"I must talk to you alone, Zelina, and somewhere where we will not be disturbed."

"I am sure that is impossible!" she said quickly.

"I insist that you listen to what I have to say."

She wondered how she could convince him that she had no wish to be alone with him. But while she was feeling for words he went on:

"I am sleeping not far from your bedroom. Tonight I will come and talk to you after everybody has gone to bed."

"No . . . no! Of course not!" Zelina exclaimed.

The Prince put his hand on her arm and she felt the strength of his fingers.

"Now listen, you foolish child. I would not do anything you would not wish me to do. I swear I will not hurt you, but I have to talk to you. I have to tell you how much you mean to me and how you thrill me as I have never been thrilled before."

"Your Highness is a . . . married man!"

"I will convince you that that is immaterial."

"You will be . . . wasting your time. "You . . . belong to your wife and to . . . nobody else."

The Prince smiled, and she knew that he was merely amused by her resistance to his suggestion. What was more, the mere fact that she was opposing him made her in his eyes even more enticing.

She was very inexperienced. At the same time, she was well aware that he desired her in a manner which was frightening.

She could almost feel his arms reaching out towards her, dragging her to him, willing her to do what he wanted in a way that was almost hypnotic.

"My door will be locked, Your Highness!" she said. "And if you come near me I shall ... scream for help, and that will ... undoubtedly cause a ... scandal."

"It is unlikely that anybody would hear you," the Prince replied, "and the scandal, my beautiful little English rose, would rest on your head, not on mine."

Zelina knew despairingly that he spoke the truth.

What she had already learnt of the Russians made her know that nobody would expect the Prince to be anything but passionate, ardent, and adventurous, and if he was found in her bedroom it was she who would be looked upon with suspicion and condemnation.

As these thoughts were going through her mind, the Prince was watching her face in a manner which Zelina felt despairingly was that of a man who was triumphantly aware that he would succeed in gaining what he desired.

"Please ... Your Highness," she pleaded impulsively, "do not ... upset or ... frighten me."

Because she was no longer fighting him, the Prince's mood changed.

"My sweet! My darling! My lovely little English rose!" he said. "I have no wish to frighten you. I want to hold you in my arms and rain kisses on your adorable face. I want to make your heart beat against mine and for us both to find that love is the only thing that matters, and the rest of the world is forgotten."

He came very close to Zelina as he spoke, and she felt as his eyes held hers that he was in fact drawing her hypnotically to him and however hard she tried it would be impossible to escape.

Then with a cry that seemed to echo round the Orangery she broke the spell by turning abruptly and, before he could prevent her, running as swiftly as her feet could carry her back down the corridor from which they had come.

She had almost reached the Salon where she had

left the Princess when a door opened just ahead of her and a man came out.

She was running so quickly that it was difficult to prevent herself from running right into him. Then as she came to a standstill she realised it was Lord Charnock.

He was staring at her curiously, and as she stood in front of him, panting from the speed at which she had run, her cheeks flushed and her hair a little dishevelled, he asked coldly:

"What are you doing? Where are you running to?"

"It . . . it is . . . the Prince!" she cried, gasping. "I am . . . afraid . . . desperately afraid of him!"

Lord Charnoock looked along the passage, saw there was nobody in sight, and taking Zelina by the arm drew her into the room he had just left.

She saw it was a room in which there were a number of bookcases, and the table in the centre of it was piled with newspapers.

There were Russian, Swedish, Polish, and Danish papers, and several English and French ones, although those were somewhat out-of-date.

For the moment Zelina was not concerned as to why Lord Charnock should be in the room. She knew only that he was there and the fear that had made her run away in terror from the Prince was now subsiding.

"What has the Prince said to upset you?" Lord Charnock enquired, and she thought he sounded angry.

"He will not . . . leave me . . . alone," Zelina said. "I . . . have . . . t-told him I . . . will not . . . listen to him because he is . . . a married man."

Lord Charnock did not speak and she went on:

"It is . . . wrong . . . very wrong for him to make . . . love to me . . . when he has a wife . . . but because he is so persistent . . . I f-find it difficult to . . . escape from him."

Lord Charnock was frowning.

"That is what I thought would happen," he said. "But why were you alone with him after what I said to you?"

"He ... asked the Princess if he could take me to ... see the Aviary," Zelina replied, "and when she agreed, I did not ... know how I could ... refuse."

Lord Charnock thought irritably that it would be almost impossible to explain to a girl of Zelina's age that a more experienced woman would somehow have found somebody to accompany her or made some plausible excuse.

He had thought when Zelina retired to bed early the night before that she had reasons for doing so which might be connected with the Prince.

Now he was wondering what he could say, what advice he could give her so that she could protect herself from his overtures.

Zelina was looking at him pleadingly.

"Please tell me ... what I can do," she said. "He seems to ... menace me, and yet I know it is ... foolish to ... feel like ... that."

"I can only tell you what I have told you before," Lord Charnock answered, "that you must not be alone with him. Go back to the Princess now and stay beside her or with one of the other ladies of the party. Some of them are near your own age. You can make new friends."

Zelina drew in her breath.

"I will ... try. I see that it was ... foolish of me, even though the Princess gave the Prince ... permission to ... take me."

"It was certainly unwise," Lord Charnock agreed.

He glanced at the clock.

"I must leave you because His Imperial Majesty is waiting to show me the carnation-houses. In fact, I came back to collect some designs for an extension of them that had been left behind."

He held up the scroll of paper he carried in his hand, and Zelina said in a voice which had a little sob in it:

"I must not . . . keep you. I realise how . . . tiresome it must be for me to keep . . . bothering you with my . . . troubles."

"They are no bother," Lord Charnock said, "but just do as I told you, and realise that everybody is aware that the Prince is outrageous in his behaviour and few people take him seriously."

Zelina did not speak, but he knew she wanted to say that whatever other people thought, she was frightened of him.

"I must go," he said quickly. "It would be a great mistake for anybody to realise that you and I have been here alone. Hurry back to the Salon where you left the Princess, and I will watch and see that nobody molests you until you get there."

Zelina thought that he was laughing at her, and she answered:

"Thank you once . . . again for being so . . . kind. I will try to be more . . . sensible another . . . time."

She did not wait for his reply but hurried down the passage. Lord Charnock watched until he saw her go into the Salon where he knew the other guests were congregated.

Then he walked to the door that led onto the terrace where the Tsar was waiting for him.

His Imperial Majesty was not really interested in carnations or in the design Lord Charnock held in his hands.

He was concentrating on a very different problem and trying to discover what was the English attitude to the Russian involvement in Turkey and Persia, and whether Lord Palmerston had any inkling of the moves they might make in the East.

Lord Charnock was perceptively aware of this, and

as he walked towards the Tsar he suddenly decided that as far as he was concerned it was a waste of time to stay much longer in Russia.

He was quite certain that, however hard he tried, he would not be able to find answers to the problems set him by Lord Palmerston, and that the Earl of Durham was managing very well to cope with any other questions that could be dealt with through diplomatic channels.

Lord Charnock had always been aware that the difficulty with the Russians was that they thought one thing and did another, and one would have to be clairvoyant to know in advance what their actions were likely to be.

"If I stayed here for the next twenty years," he told himself, "I would get no further."

On the other hand, some chance remark made indiscreetly might reveal a whole new chain of circumstances which would be exactly what Lord Palmerston wished to know.

"It is too difficult," he told himself, "and I really have something better to do with my life than dance attendance on Monarchs, however powerful they may be."

He had decided since he had come to Russia that he positively disliked the Tsar, and there were plenty of people ready to tell him of the more alarming features of His Majesty's character.

These included his tendency to declare people insane if they did not agree with him, and his Department, known as the Third Section of the Secret Police, whose whole function under his friend Count Benckendorff was to act as the nation's moral physician in every town in Russia.

What angered Lord Charnock more than anything else was the prevalent poverty, sickness, and privation amongst the ordinary people.

While a thousand guests were entertained at supper in the Winter Palace, women and children were dying of starvation, and the Tsar was designing more extravagant and more expensive "peacock" uniforms for his troops.

"The whole thing is a crazy farce!" Lord Charnock said to himself. "And the sooner I return to the sanity of England, the better!"

Accordingly, while he handed over the designs he had fetched for the Tsar, he asked him almost abruptly questions which no Diplomat would have dared to put into words.

For some strange reason, the Tsar, instead of crushing him as he was quite capable of doing, answered Lord Charnock frankly, openly revealing his interest in Persia but declaring that he had no wish to do anything that the British would dislike.

When it was time for luncheon the Tsar and Lord Charnock were in such close accord that they walked back to the Palace with His Imperial Majesty's arm through that of the Englishman.

Vaguely, even though his thoughts were fully occupied with his diplomatic success, Lord Charnock noticed that Zelina seemed quite happy and was talking animatedly to the gentleman sitting next to her at the table.

When the luncheon was over the Tsar once again demanded Lord Charnock's company, and they talked together for the rest of the afternoon until it was time to dress for dinner.

When the meal was over the Tsarina announced that there was a special entertainment to amuse the guests, and they went from the Dining-Room to a large Salon where there was a terrace overlooking one of the many ornamental gardens.

A number of chairs had been arranged on the terrace and the guests occupying them were sheltered from any night-winds by screens and banks of flowers.

However, it was a still, warm night, but even so the servants brought rugs of ermine and sable for the ladies, and there were also wraps of the same beautiful furs should they feel in the least cold.

Then, under the stars that were just beginning to rise in the sky, the gypsy dancers appeared and their heart-stirring music filled the air.

It was very different from the dancing Zelina had watched aboard the *Ischora*.

The gypsy women in their brilliantly colourful skirts and gold jewellery were as exotic and as attractive as she had expected them to be.

They twirled and leapt in the air, and spun round with a wild, uncontrolled exuberance that, like the music, roused the senses and made Zelina's heart beat with the rhythm of their movements and their voices.

It was all so exciting and exhilarating that she felt as if the gypsies swept her out of herself and into a primitive world of wonder and delight where her spirit was free from constrictions and constraint.

She wanted to sing, to dance, to fly into the sky and touch the stars.

Then as she felt herself throbbing with the excitement of it, she realised with a little stab of fear that the Prince was watching her.

She wished she could have hidden her feelings from him, for she felt almost as if he intruded on something that was very private.

The gypsies' performance lasted for two hours, and when it was over it seemed as if they had raised everybody's spirits, for they laughed, talked, and drank, and it was quite late before the Tsar and Tsarina retired and everybody else was able to go to bed.

"I am sure you have enjoyed yourself, Zelina," the Princess said as they went up the stairs together.

"It has been wonderful!" Zelina answered. "I always thought the gypsies would be like that."

"I am glad you are not disappointed," the Princess said with a smile. "Our Russian gypsies are very talented. In fact, some of our greatest Ballerinas have gypsy blood in them."

"I do hope I shall see them again."

"You will, I promise you," the Princess replied.

They reached the door of Zelina's room, which was some way from the Princess's Suite, which was almost at the end of the long corridor.

Princess Olga bent to kiss Zelina's cheek.

"Good-night, my dear," she said. "You have been very much admired tonight, especially by Prince Alexis. He is enraptured by your beauty!"

Zelina was about to reply that it was the last thing she wanted, but the Princess had already moved away and there was nothing she could do but go into her own room.

She opened the door, and as she was still throbbing with the wonder of the dancing she went to the window to open it and look up at the sky.

Russia was strange and unpredictable, she thought, and yet it was also very interesting.

It would have been impossible not to be impressed with the magnificence of the Palaces, the amazing treasures she had seen in every room, and of course the Tsar and Tsarina themselves.

Then as Zelina looked at the stars twinkling overhead she felt that in a way she could understand that the gypsies aroused in people feelings that were part of love.

Perhaps love was overwhelming, irresistible, omnipotent.

Yet she was sure when she thought about it that the love which Prince Alexis talked about was very different from the love she wanted.

The love she would give the man of her heart was like a shining star in her mind, and it was not only wild and exciting but tender, kind, and compassionate.

"I want love that will make me feel safe," Zelina told herself.

Then, like a blinding light coming from the stars at which she was gazing, she knew the answer.

The love she yearned for, the love that she could feel beating within her breast, was what she felt for Lord Charnock.

She had been very foolish not to recognise it before, when to talk to him had been so exciting and had made her feel as if she belonged to him.

When he was there she was no longer frightened but was content in a way which she could not explain.

Her love seemed now to sweep over her with a joy and a rapture that made her want to cling to him and never leave him.

"I love him!" she said finally, and heard the surprise in her own voice.

She stood for a long time looking up at the Heavens. Then she told herself that she must undress and go to bed, when almost like a vision of the serpent entering the Garden of Eden she remembered Prince Alexis.

Quickly, because she was instantly terrified, she went to the door.

She would lock herself in, and however hard he tried he would not reach her.

She put out her hand to turn the key.

Then she was still, as if she had been turned to stone, shocked to find that the key was missing.

Chapter Six

Zelina felt panic sweeping over her like a flood-tide.

She wanted to scream, she wanted to escape from the Palace, from Russia, from everything that was menacing her like some giant ogre.

Then she remembered that if she made a scene, it was she who would be considered reprehensible, not the Prince.

He had said that his bedroom was near to hers, and she thought frantically that if she knew where Lord Charnock was sleeping she would go to him, but she had no idea where he might be in the vast Palace.

"What shall I do? Oh, God, what shall I do?" she asked.

Then she remembered something strange that had happened when her maid had been unpacking for her.

The room in which she was sleeping had panelled walls like many of the other rooms in the Palace.

They were painted white and picked out in gold which matched the elaborate cornice and the ornamental ceiling.

However, there was no wardrobe in the room, and the Russian maid obviously thought that the panelling concealed a cupboard.

She walked from the trunk carrying one of Zelina's gowns over her arm and touched one of the elaborately carved panels.

Zelina saw it fly open and was surprised to see how

narrow it was and that the aperture it revealed was very small.

She was just about to say that she would not be able to fit many of her gowns in there, when she saw an expression of terror on the maid's face.

She muttered something in Russian, then crossed herself.

It was then that Zelina understood that what the maid had found inadvertently was a secret hiding-place.

The maid would have closed the panelling again, but Zelina moved forward and prevented her.

She had heard about secret hiding-places in Russian Palaces and thought they must be something like the Priest-holes which were to be found in many of the Elizabethan houses in England.

"Let me look," she said. "I want to see how the mechanism works."

"Non, non, M'mselle!" the maid protested in broken French. "Very dangerous look. Much trouble for me!"

"I promise I will tell nobody," Zelina answered.

As if she was too frightened to look at what she had revealed, the maid rushed to the other side of the room and opened some other panelling which swung back to show what she had expected to find in the first place—a cupboard.

There was plenty of room in it not only for Zelina's gowns but also for her trunk, but she was sure that if she hid there the Prince would find her.

Instead she ran across the room to search the place in the carving where the pressure of her fingers would open the secret hiding-place.

For a moment she thought desperately that it would not work. Then the panel swung back and she slipped into the dark aperture, and she was just about to close the panel behind her when she had another idea.

By the light from the candles on her dressing-table and from the candelabra on the chest-of-drawers she could see that there was an entrance from the hiding-place not only into her bedroom but also into the bedroom next door.

Zelina was almost sure this was empty, but she opened the panel slowly and very carefully just in case she was mistaken.

By the light from the stars through the uncurtained window she saw that the room was empty and the bed not turned down.

Quickly she closed the opening into her own bedroom, then the one behind her.

'I am safe!' she thought with a little sigh of relief.

Then, because her fear of the Prince was still with her, she wondered if he knew the secrets of the Palace and would perhaps guess how she was able to elude him.

'I will not stay here,' she thought. 'I will go still farther on.'

She guessed that whoever had designed the secret entrances would perhaps have made them the same in quite a number of the rooms.

It took her a little time to find one in the room where she now was, but her fingers found the same place in a carved flower, and as the panel opened slowly and silently she thought with a leap of her heart that she had been very clever.

She stepped into the darkness of the hiding-place and as she did so she heard someone speak.

The room beyond was occupied!

"May I come in, Count?" a man's voice asked in French. "I have a message from His Imperial Majesty."

"Yes, of course, Philippe," was the reply. "I rather hoped there would be such news after the Tsar spent so much time with Lord Charnock. Sit down and tell me what has happened."

"His Majesty is very pleased with himself," the man called Philippe replied. "He is quite certain that Charnock has no idea that we are concerned with anything except Turkey and Persia."

"His Majesty is sure of that?" the Count asked.

"Quite certain! We can therefore go ahead with our plans to infiltrate into Afghanistan."

"Good! That makes everything very much easier than I expected."

Because of what was being said and because Lord Charnock's name had been mentioned, Zelina knew that if the two men talking were aware that she had overheard their conversation, her life would undoubtedly be in danger.

She had the idea that the man who had been addressed as "Count" was Count Karl Robert Nesselrode, the Russian Minister for Foreign Affairs, and she knew from the way everybody in the party deferred to him that he was without doubt of great importance.

She had an idea, from what she had read in the newspapers, that it was the Count with whom Lord Palmerston negotiated.

But she was so frightened that she did not dare move except very, very cautiously to close the panel that opened into the empty bedroom behind her.

Then she could only stand listening to everything that was said in the bedroom beyond, praying that by no unwary movement or sound would the two men talking suspect that they were being overheard.

Strangely enough, she did not feel suffocated though confined in such a small space, and she was sure that the hiding-places received enough fresh air for whoever was listening to be able to do so indefinitely.

Only when the Count and Philippe had at last said good-night, and Count Nesselrode, if that was who he was, had got into bed and was snoring loudly, was

Zelina able to slip from her hiding-place back into the empty bedroom.

She thought that by now if the Prince had visited her he would have gone away, but she was far too frightened to risk returning to discover whether or not he had waited for her.

Instead, she locked the outside door of the bedroom she was in, and because by now she was almost dropping with fatigue she lay down on the bed and tried to sleep.

It was actually nearly dawn before she managed to drift away into a restless slumber.

When a little later the sunshine coming through the uncurtained window awakened her, she thought it would be safe to return to her own room.

She went back through the secret passage.

The room looked exactly as she had left it, but all the same she felt that the Prince had been there.

It was as if he had left an angry, frustrated vibration in the air, but because in the daylight nothing was quite so terrifying as it had been the night before, Zelina undressed and got into bed.

She did not ring for her maid until much later in the morning, then having eaten the breakfast which was brought her on a tray, she rose, dressed and went downstairs.

She knew she had to find Lord Charnock and not only relate to him what she had overheard the night before, but also tell him that she could not protect herself against the Prince.

The Palace seemed even larger than it had the day before and it was difficult to know where Lord Charnock would be or how she could see him alone.

Now that she knew of the secret hiding-places in the bedroom she was well aware that it would be impossible for her to talk to him in any of the Sitting-Rooms without the risk of being overheard.

"When I find him," she told herself, "I must ask him to come with me into the garden."

She looked into one of two of the Salons but they were empty.

Then as she stood irresolutely looking at the table covered with newspapers, the door slammed shut behind her and she turned round to see the Prince.

One look at his face was enough to tell her how angry he was, and Zelina could only stare at him, her eyes wide with fear as he walked slowly towards her.

"Where have you been?" he asked furiously. "Where were you last night?"

He put out his hand as he spoke and took hold of her arm above the elbow, digging his fingers painfully into the softness of her skin.

"If you were with Charnock, I think I will kill you!" he said. "I believed you were pure and innocent, but now I am suspicious and I want an explanation of where you were hiding from me."

With an effort Zelina found her voice.

"Y-you have no right to . . . ask me such questions . . . Your Highness!"

She tried to speak in a dignified, haughty manner, but her voice quivered, and because he was so close to her she was trembling.

"I want an answer to my question, and you will give it to me, if I have to beat it out of you!" the Prince roared. "Where were you?"

"I was somewhere . . . safe where you . . . could not . . . find me, and I was . . . alone."

She told herself that Lord Charnock must not be involved in this because the Prince might harm him, and she was aware when she said the word "alone" that some of the anger seemed to go from his face.

Now he was looking at her searchingly.

"Is that true?"

He was still holding her arm, but not so painfully.

"There is no . . . reason for me to . . . lie, Your Highness, and if you . . . came to my room it was a . . . despicable action and . . . something you had no . . . right to do!"

"I have every right, because I love you," the Prince replied. "You are mine, Zelina, and I swear that no other man shall touch you!"

He took his hand from her arm as he spoke, but only so that he could pull her roughly against him.

She gave a cry of sheer terror, then as she turned her head away because she thought he was about to kiss her, she felt his lips, hot and burning, on her neck.

This frightened her more and more, and the insistence of his mouth made her feel as if he had captured her as he intended and she would never be able to escape him.

She tried to fight herself free of him, but she was imprisoned in his arms and he went on kissing the softness of her neck and the line of her chin until his lips were on her cheek.

She knew that struggle as she might, he would take possession of her lips, when as she gave a stifled scream the door of the room opened and one of the Tsar's *Aides-de-Camp* came in.

He was wearing an elaborate red-coated uniform, heavily gold-braided, which the Tsar had designed himself. As a soldier he was too well trained to show any surprise at the scene being enacted before him.

The Prince, however, raised his head to ask furiously:

"What the devil do you want?"

"Your pardon, Your Highness," the *Aide-de-Camp* replied, "but I have been trying to find Miss Tiverton. I have a message for her from Lord Charnock."

Because the Prince's arms had relaxed a little Zelina was able to extricate herself, and she moved quickly towards the *Aide-de-Camp*, saying in a voice that did not sound like her own:

"You . . . have a . . . message for . . . me?"

"Yes, Miss Tiverton. Lord Charnock asked me to inform you that he is leaving in an hour's time for St. Petersburg, from where he is returning to England."

Zelina gave a gasp, then moved past the *Aide-de-Camp* through the door into the passage, saying as she went:

"I must . . . go to . . . Lord Charnock . . . at once. Tell me . . . where I can . . . find him."

She had escaped from the Prince, and she had proceeded quite a long way down the passage before the *Aide-de-Camp* caught up with her.

"Where is His . . . Lordship?" Zelina asked, her breath coming fitfully between her lips.

"I am afraid, Miss Tiverton," he replied, "you cannot speak to His Lordship at the moment because he is in conference with His Imperial Majesty and cannot be disturbed."

Zelina stopped.

"I *must* . . . speak to . . . him!" she said, more to herself than to the *Aide-de-Camp*.

"I am sure you will be able to do so," he replied. "His Lordship will make his farewells to Her Majesty the Tsarina in the Salon Vert, and if you will wait there, there will be no chance of your missing him."

Zelina was aware that in these circumstances it would be impossible to talk to Lord Charnock intimately and without being overheard.

She wanted to scream to the *Aide-de-Camp* that she must see him alone. Then she had a sudden idea.

It took a few seconds for it to formulate in her mind, and she was aware that the *Aide-de-Camp* was waiting patiently, watching her curiously as he did so.

"Will you tell His Lordship . . . when you . . . see him," she said at length, "that I deeply . . . regret I am unable to say . . . good-bye to him, and I wish him . . . . 'Bon Voyage' and a . . . safe return to England."

"I will of course convey your message, Miss Tiverton," the *Aide-de-Camp* replied.

"Thank you," Zelina answered.

Without saying any more, she turned and ran as swiftly as her feet could carry her back along the passage and up the stairs to her bedroom.

It did not take her long to change into her riding-habit, and when she was ready she sent the maid downstairs to order a horse for her to ride.

"I do not wish to be accompanied when I am riding," she said to the maid, "except of course by a groom, so please ask for the horse to be somewhere where I am unlikely to be seen leaving the Palace."

"I understand, *M'mselle,*" the maid replied.

She came back a little while later to escort Zelina by a devious route to a side-door where there was nobody about and only two sentries on guard.

A magnificent jet-black stallion was waiting for her and also a groom with another superlative animal, which, like all the horses in the Royal Stables, was trained to move faster than any English horse Zelina had ever ridden.

The groom in attendance in his elaborate livery was an intelligent man who spoke a little French, enough at any rate for him to understand where she wished to go.

Then they set off at a breathtaking pace through the Park-land that encircled the Palace and out into the countryside towards the road which led to St. Petersburg.

*   *   *

Lord Charnock spent a restless night thinking how he could leave without causing offence.

After his long interview with the Tsar he decided that there was nothing further to keep him in Russia, and he was quite certain that however long he went on talking and discussing the subject of Persia and Turkey, he would learn no more.

His perception, which was never at fault, told him that the Tsar was keeping back from him the information which Lord Palmerston was so anxious to know.

Yet he was sure that there was no chance of His Majesty letting slip anything that was not already known to the British, and that to continue optimistically hoping for a revelation was a sheer waste of time.

Lord Charnock also knew that the geniality which the Tsar had shown to him so far was quite likely to change at any moment to a very different mood.

Nobody was more unpredictable or more unbalanced than Tsar Nicholas, and everybody he talked to made Lord Charnock aware that he walked a tight-rope where one unwary step might precipitate him into disaster.

It was exceedingly important that the Tsar's anxiety to co-operate with the British should not change, and Lord Charnock's instinct told him that he would be well advised to leave before his good-will was exhausted.

He also had a personal reason for wishing to go, and that was a simple one: he was bored with the demands that the Countess Natasha was making on him.

He was far too astute not to know that what had been originally a job to be done with the expertise for which she was famous had turned into something different for her.

Lord Charnock was used to the women to whom he made love becoming infatuated with him, but with the Countess Natasha it was something wilder and deeper than the desire of a woman for a competent lover.

Perhaps because some of the men she had seduced at the command of the Tsar had not been particularly attractive, she had found Lord Charnock so alluring that she had to all intents and purposes lost her head.

"I love you!" she had said a thousand times both in French and English, and it had been impossible for him not to hear the sincerity in her voice.

He doubted cynically if she knew the meaning of real love, but he could not fail to be aware that she was obsessed with a heart-throbbing, overwhelming passion which with the Russians was something uncontrolled and primitive.

Because she was very beautiful and skilled at all the exotic arts of love-making known to the Orient, Lord Charnock did not find it difficult to comply with her demands.

At the same time, it was with a sense of relief that he had found that the Countess was not included amongst the guests at Tsarskoye Selo.

Then last night when the Tsar was retiring to bed with his bird-like Prussian wife Alexandra, whom he adored, he had said:

"If you feel lonely after listening to the gypsy music, tomorrow Natasha Obolensky will be joining us."

He spoke as if he were presenting Lord Charnock with a special favour, and there was nothing the latter could do but express his gratitude.

The Tsar had then offered his arm to his wife and escorted her from the Salon as the ladies swept down in deep curtseys and the gentlemen bowed their heads from the neck.

In his own room Lord Charnock was thankful that tonight at any rate he could sleep without being disturbed and any secret entrances would remain closed.

He had decided that somehow he must find an excuse to leave, and it seemed almost like the answer to a prayer when this morning while he was having breakfast with the gentlemen in the party a servant came to his side to inform him that a messenger had arrived from the British Ambassador in St. Petersburg.

Lord Charnock had seen the man in one of the private rooms allotted for such purposes, where he was quite certain everything that was said would be overheard.

"His Excellency the Earl of Durham has asked me, My Lord," the messenger said, "to give this personal letter into your hands and to inform you when you have read it that His Majesty's ship *Dolphin* is in the harbour."

Lord Charnock looked at the messenger with speculative eyes but said nothing. He merely opened the heavily sealed letter that was handed to him.

Inside the envelope was another one, and when he had opened it Lord Charnock recognised the upright, rather large writing of Lord Palmerston.

He sat down in a chair to read it carefully.

> *My dear Charnock:*
>   *It is with deep regret that I write to inform you that your mother is unwell.*
>   *Her Physicians in attendance think it wise for you to return as soon as possible to be with her.*
>   *I can only convey to you my deepest sympathy and hope this letter does not arrive at an inconvenient time or interfere with the pleasantries of your visit.*
>   *To make it possible for you to travel as swiftly as possible, I have sent this letter in the care of the Captain of the H.M.S. Dolphin, who will await your instructions.*
>
>   *I remain,*
>   *Yours most sincerely,*
>   *Palmerston.*

Lord Charnock finished reading the letter and saw that at the bottom there was a "P.S." in code.

Because it was one he most frequently used, he could decipher it easily, and he read:

> *Do not worry unduly about your mother.*

Lord Charnock knew then that his mother, to whom he was deeply attached, was not in any danger.

However, she was never in very good health, and this was an excuse which had often been used to facilitate his departure from countries or situations which had become untenable.

Now he knew with a feeling of satisfaction that this was exactly the excuse he required, and he said to the messenger:

"What vehicles have brought you here?"

"Two carriages, My Lord."

Lord Charnock smiled.

He knew that meant that the Earl of Durham was aware that he would leave as soon as he had read the letter from Lord Palmerston.

"You had better first have some breakfast," he said to the messenger, "and we will leave in an hour."

"Very good, My Lord."

Lord Charnock went to find an *Aide-de-Camp* to ask first if he might have an interview with the Tsar, and secondly to convey a message to Zelina.

He had not forgotten his promise that he would not leave without telling her.

However, he was annoyed when he learnt that she had just sent him a message of farewell and not come as he had expected to say good-bye.

'I wanted to see her,' he thought as he drove away from the Palace.

He was relieved to go, but at the same time he was apprehensive at leaving Zelina behind.

Then he told himself that there was no need for him to worry about her. After all, the Princess would look after her, and sooner or later she would have to stand on her own feet.

Nevertheless, he found himself thinking that it was a lesson which would be easier for her to learn in England than in Russia.

He was frowning as the four horses drawing the carriage in which he was travelling gathered speed.

There was only one road from St. Petersburg to Tsarskoye Selo, and because it was used by the Tsar it was undoubtedly the best in Russia, and very different from the pot-holed, dusty, or muddy tracks in other parts of the country.

These usually resulted in most travellers being delayed for hours or even days on their journey.

The countryside in the sunshine was looking particularly beautiful, but Lord Charnock was thinking of Zelina and wondering how she could have been content to let him leave without saying farewell.

Her eyes were very expressive and he was too experienced not to suspect that she had begun to feel for him not only because he stood for safety and security but also because she was aware of him as a man.

Not that he thought for a moment that she was in love with him, but that ever since they had travelled together in first the English ship and then the *Ischora* he had begun to mean something in her life.

"That is only because she is so young, and the world is a frightening place," Lord Charnock told himself.

Then he was thinking that the Countess Natasha's sensuous love-making and the way, sinuously like a serpent, she entwined herself round him had made him feel it would be almost impossible to free himself of her clinging arms.

Now he knew he would never see her again, at least he hoped not, but the Russians were always unpredictable, and when they were in love they could behave in an entirely uncivilised manner for which there was no precedent.

This made him think of the Prince, and there was a heavy scowl on Lord Charnock's forehead.

He thought he should have insisted on seeing Zelina and perhaps have waited for her.

At least he should have told her that if the Prince became too uncontrollable she could ask the British Ambassador to arrange for her to return home.

'I suppose she has enough money,' he thought and decided that the moment he arrived in St. Petersburg he would write a letter to her telling her what she could do.

At the same time, he would alert the Ambassador of the situation in which she found herself.

He did not particularly want the Earl to be aware of his concern about Zelina, but it was extremely important that the child should be looked after and not upset by Prince Alexis, whose name was a byword for indiscretion and impropriety.

"Damn the man!" Lord Charnock said beneath his breath. "I should have dealt with him before I left!"

It was then, as he was berating himself for being so glad to get away and for not troubling about Zelina, that he realised the horses were slowing down.

As they were in the middle of open country he thought it strange. Then as he looked ahead he saw that the coachman was drawing in his reins because there were two people on horse-back in the centre of the road ahead.

He wondered vaguely what was the matter, until as the horses finally came to a stop somebody rode up to the side of the carriage and he saw who it was.

"Zelina!" he exclaimed.

She bent forward from her saddle to say to him:

"I had to speak to you ... alone, and this was the ... only way I could do so."

She was very pale, and her eyes, which were unnaturally large in her small face, seemed to be beseeching him.

Lord Charnock smiled.

"Of course."

He was aware what she had to say must not be overheard by the coachman or the footman on the box of the carriage.

It was unusual for any of the servants, except for personal staff and those who were in the employment of the British Embassy, to speak anything but Russian, but one never knew for certain.

It was quite possible that the footman was trained to listen to what was said behind him in an open carriage, and of course to report it to the Secret Police, who were everywhere.

"I suggest," Lord Charnock said, "that we take a little walk. As it is a nice day, I shall enjoy stretching my legs."

Zelina flashed him a smile as if she was glad that he had understood, and as she dismounted from her horse, Lord Charnock signalled to the footman to open the door of the carriage, then he stepped out.

Zelina went to his side and they walked away through the flower-filled grass towards a clump of trees which would protect them from the sun.

There they could look back and see the two carriages drawn up one behind the other; the second, containing the messenger from the British Embassy and Hibbert, was closed because Lord Charnock's trunks were piled on top of it.

He did not speak until they reached the trees, and then as Zelina looked up at him nervously, he asked:

"What is all this about? I wondered why you did not wish me farewell with the rest of the party."

"I . . . I had to see you . . . alone."

Her voice was tense and a little hoarse, and she added before Lord Charnock could speak:

"Is it true that you are . . . leaving for . . . England?"

"I have received a message that my mother is ill."

"I am sorry to hear that," Zelina said, "but you cannot leave me . . . here."

As she spoke, she saw that this was what Lord Charnock had anticipated she might say, and as his lips moved and she was sure he was going to tell her that there was nothing he could do about it, she said quickly:

"The Prince . . . came to my bedroom . . . last night!"

Lord Charnock stiffened and she went on:

"He had taken away the key, and because I was so desperately . . . frightened, I managed to escape through a . . . secret panel in the wall into the . . . next-door bedroom."

"Are you sure the Prince took the key from your room?" Lord Charnock asked.

"Quite sure!" Zelina answered. "He told me he was . . . coming to talk to me. Then when I was determined I would . . . lock him out, I found I was . . . unable to do so."

"This is disgraceful! Despicable!" Lord Charnock ejaculated.

"It was fortunate that my maid by . . . mistake showed me a . . . secret entrance," Zelina said, "but to be quite certain that the Prince would not find me, I looked for another in the . . . empty room next to mine, and . . . I found one!"

"That was clever of you!"

"It saved me," she said simply, "and when I was in the second secret hiding-place I overheard a . . . conversation in the room beyond, which was occupied, and it . . . concerned you!"

Lord Charnock did not speak, but she knew he was listening attentively and she said:

"I think, although I am not sure, that the man who was sleeping in that room was Count Nesselrode, and the other man he addressed as 'Philippe.'"

"That would be Baron Philippe de Brunnow," Lord Charnock said. "He is the *Premier Redacteur* for the Ministry of Foreign Affairs."

"The Tsar sent him with a message to Count Nesselrode after he had talked to you."

"And you heard what was said?"

Zelina saw by the sudden alertness in Lord Charnock's eyes that this was of vital interest to him.

She nodded.

"Will you tell me what you heard?"

"I thought you would want to know," she replied, "and I have tried to remember every word."

"Thank you, Zelina," Lord Charnock said. "Now tell me what it was."

Slowly and carefully Zelina repeated the Tsar's message and what Count Nesselrode had said to Baron de Brunnow. Then she went on:

"They continued talking about India."

"Go on," Lord Charnock prompted as she paused.

"Count Nesselrode said," she continued, "'India is separated from Russia by two thousand miles of territory belonging to Persia, Afghanistan, and the Independent Sikh State of the Punjab. Lord Palmerston is determined to do all he can to prevent this distance from being shortened, but he will be disappointed.' "

As she spoke she looked at Lord Charnock and saw his lips tighten.

Then she ended:

"They both laughed."

There was a moment's silence before Lord Charnock said:

"Thank you, Zelina. As I am sure you are aware, the information you have given me is of vital importance, but you took a great risk in listening to it."

"I thought when I was in the secret place which had been made inside the walls of the room that if I was . . . discovered, they might wish to . . . dispose of me."

"I am quite certain," Lord Charnock said, "that you would have had an 'unfortunate accident.'"

"But there is no reason for them to think they had been overheard," Zelina said. "At the same time, it makes me afraid . . . but not as . . . afraid as I am of the . . . Prince."

She clasped her hands together as she said:

"Oh, Lord Charnock, please . . . please take me home with you! I cannot . . . stay behind and know that he is . . . determined to make me his . . . mistress!"

She spoke the last word almost in a whisper, and her voice broke.

It seemed to her so degrading, so humiliating that a man should want her not as his wife but as the sort of woman of whom her mother would not even have spoken.

Lord Charnock was silent, and Zelina's eyes filled with tears as she begged:

"Please . . . please . . . if you are not there . . . I think it will be . . . impossible for me to . . . save myself."

Lord Charnock smiled.

"I think, Zelina, you and I should proceed to St. Petersburg with all possible speed!"

He saw her stare at him as if she could hardly believe what she had heard, then there was a sudden light in her eyes and the colour came into her cheeks.

"I . . . I can . . . come with . . . you?" she asked, as if she was afraid she had misunderstood what he had said.

"I will send a message with your groom."

As he spoke he turned to walk back the way they had come and Zelina moved beside him without speaking.

As she stepped into his carriage, Lord Charnock instructed her groom to return to the Palace, taking with him the horse she had been riding, and to inform the Princess Volkonsky that Miss Tiverton was travelling with him to the British Embassy in St. Petersburg.

The groom appeared to understand, and when Lord Charnock got into the carriage he signalled his coachman to move on. The horses started off on the smooth road at a pace which almost blew Zelina's riding-hat from her head.

She clutched it in one hand and turned to Lord Charnock to say:

"Thank you . . . thank you! I was so . . . afraid that you would . . . send me back."

As she spoke, she slipped her other hand under the rug and into his.

She had taken off her glove and her fingers were cold. They were also trembling, but he was aware that it was not with fear but with excitement and a happiness which had swept away even the horrors of the previous night.

Then as Lord Charnock's fingers closed over hers, he knew what he must do.

Because they were travelling so fast it was difficult to speak, and only as they reached the traffic outside St. Petersburg did Zelina ask with a note of anxiety in her voice:

"You . . . will take me . . . back to England with . . . you?"

"You are quite certain you do not wish to see any more of Russia?"

"I do not wish even to think about it again!" Zelina retorted.

She tightened her hold on Lord Charnock as if she was afraid that at the last moment he would leave her behind.

They were now driving alongside the Neva, and as Lord Charnock looked at the shining spires and golden domes ahead he said:

"So much beauty and so much waste and cruelty! A country of violent contrasts!"

Then he asked in a very much more practical tone:

"What about your clothes?"

"I have several trunks at the Palace," Zelina replied, "and what I have left behind is of no consequence, or perhaps they might send them after me."

"I think that unlikely," he remarked drily.

He bent forward and gave directions to the coach-man, who was now travelling more slowly, and a few minutes later they stopped outside the Volkonsky Palace.

As they did so, Zelina looked up at Lord Charnock enquiringly.

"What I want you to do," he said, "is to go in, change, and be ready to leave when I return for you."

"Y-you will not be ... long?"

"The British Embassy is not far away," he said. "I will be less than half-an-hour."

"I will not keep you waiting."

She took her fingers from his hand reluctantly, as if she was afraid to let him go, and said:

"You are quite ... quite certain you will ... come back? You will not ... change your mind?"

"I promise I will be here at the time you expect me," he said quietly.

"I will be ready!"

She ran in through the open front door of the palace as the carriage drove away.

"I must not keep him waiting!" she told herself as she hurried upstairs.

She knew that what was really frightening her was the thought that in some unexpected manner Lord Charnock would be prevented from coming to fetch her or she would be unable to leave the Palace.

It was impossible to think how this could happen, and yet Zelina was sure, although she had no logical reason for thinking it, that Prince Alexis in some devious way of his own would try to keep her in Russia.

"Please, God . . . look after Lord Charnock and let us get . . . away," she prayed.

Then as there was no time to lose she reached her own bedroom and was sending for the housemaids to help her change and to see that her trunks were conveyed downstairs to wait for Lord Charnock's return.

"Hurry! Hurry! Hurry!" she cried to the maids, and knew that her heart was saying the same thing.

Chapter Seven

Because Zelina was in such a hurry, she put on the first gown that the maids took from the top of one of her trunks.

Only when it was being fastened and the bonnet that matched it was brought to her at the dressing-table did she realise it was one of the smartest afternoon-gowns she possessed.

Of pink crepe, it was decorated round the hem with row upon row of lace and there was lace on the sleeves and round the neck.

The pink ribbons which crossed over her breasts and which matched the ribbons on her bonnet together with the roses on the crown made her look like the English rose which Prince Alexis had called her so often in his endearments.

For a moment she shuddered at the thought of him and considered changing the gown.

Then she knew it was very becoming, and it was far more important that she should look her best for Lord Charnock than worry about the Prince.

Time was passing and she had the frightened feeling that perhaps when Prince Alexis found she had left Tsarskoye Selo he would follow her to St. Petersburg and prevent her from leaving Russia.

Because the idea terrified her, she left her bed-room and ran down the stairs to see if Lord Charnock had returned.

She knew it was too soon for him to have done so,

and yet every minute she was not with him seemed full
of indescribable danger.

Because the servants in the Hall looked at her
curiously, she went into the nearest Salon, and for once
the magnificent treasures it contained—the paintings,
the objets d'art, and the exquisitely painted ceiling—
were of no interest.

All she wanted was the security of England, and
the shabby rooms in what had been her home seemed
far more beautiful than anything the Palaces could offer.

Then she thought of Lord Charnock and was
suddenly aware that she had only been thinking of
herself and not of him.

She was not so foolish as not to be aware that for
him to travel back to England with a young, unchaperoned
girl would undoubtedly cause a scandal.

He had been so careful in managing to contrive
that she arrived in St. Petersburg with a lady's-maid
borrowed from the British Minister's wife in Copenhagen.

He had made it seem to the Russians that his
entire interest in her had been that she was English
and her uncle and aunt were well known in Society.

It would be very different if she travelled with him
on his return journey without another woman and with
no reasonable explanation except that she wished to
leave Russia.

"What shall I do? What can I do?" she asked
herself.

Because she loved him she felt that she must not
harm him in any way, and she was sure that the
whispers of women like her aunt and their unkind
laughter would not only be embarrassing for him but
might damage his political life.

"What can I do?" she asked herself again, and
thought that if her love was great enough she would
return to Tsarskoye Selo and face the Prince.

Even as she knew that if she did so he would force

himself upon her and she would be unable to defend herself, Lord Charnock walked into the Salon.

She gave a little cry at the sight of him!

Then, when she would have said what was in her mind, she remembered that even in the Volkonsky Palace there doubtless were spies who would overhear what they said to each other.

"Are you ready?" Lord Charnock asked.

"Yes," she answered, "but there is something I must say to you . . . but not . . . here."

She saw that he understood what she implied, and he merely remarked:

"A carriage is outside and one for your luggage."

Zelina moved ahead and, leaving the Salon, walked across the Hall towards the front door.

As she walked over the carpet which had now been laid on the steps to the pavement to where the British Embassy carriage was waiting, she saw her trunks being loaded onto the carriage behind.

It flashed through her mind that they might have to be brought back again. Then as Lord Charnock sat down beside her, a footman closed the carriage-door and the horses moved off.

The vehicle they were travelling in now was closed, and Zelina supposed it was because Lord Charnock did not want anybody to see them travelling together.

Quickly she said to him:

"Before you take me to the ship . . . there is something I must . . . say to you."

"We are going first to the British Embassy," Lord Charnock replied, "and then I will listen to anything you have to say."

He spoke very gently, as if he knew that she was upset, and they sat in silence as the horses trotted through the wide streets designed by Tsar Peter.

It was only a short distance to the British Embassy,

and the servants waiting at the front door were obviously expecting them.

"Will you tell His Excellency we are here?" Lord Charnock asked the Butler. "Miss Tiverton and I would like to wait in the small Drawing-Room."

The Butler walked ahead of them across the marble Hall to open the door.

The Drawing-Room into which they were shown looked to Zelina very English in its design and furnishings, and that in itself was somehow comforting because it was such a contrast to the opulent manificence of the Russian Palaces.

Then, intent only on what she had to say to Lord Charnock, she looked up at him with an expression in her eyes which he could not for the moment interpret.

"What has happened? What has upset you?" he asked.

"I . . . I have been . . . thinking," she replied, "and there is . . . something which you must consider before we . . . leave."

"What is that?"

"You have been so kind, so unbelievably and incredibly kind in saying you will take me away from Russia. But you must think of yourself . . . and your career . . . and that for me to travel . . . alone with you to England might . . . harm you."

"You are thinking of me?" Lord Charnock asked with an incredulous note in his voice.

"Yes, of course," Zelina replied. "And because you are so . . . important and everybody . . . respects you, I cannot have people saying unkind things which, although they are untrue, would . . . as you well know . . . damage your career."

"I understand what you are saying to me," Lord Charnock replied, "and I am very touched. At the same time, there is no alternative."

"I have . . . thought of one . . . if you will . . . agree."

"And what is that?"

"If you will please take me to the first port that is outside Russia, I could . . . find my own way home from . . . there. Then, if you speak to the Captain of the ship, nobody need know I have . . . been with you."

Zelina did not look at Lord Charnock as she spoke, afraid that she might see in his eyes the relief that he would be rid of her.

There was a moment's silence. Then he said:

"You are really suggesting that to save my good name you are willing to brave the dangers of travelling back to England alone?"

"It . . . it does . . . frighten me," Zelina admitted, "but now that I know what to . . . expect . . . I will stay in my cabin, and if there were any men like . . . Mr. Adamson aboard they would not . . . see me."

"Why does it concern you so deeply that people should not gossip about me?" Lord Charnock enquired.

"Because you are of such vital . . . importance," Zelina explained. "I do not know why you were . . . sent to Russia, but the Tsar, Count Nesselrode, and of course Lord Palmerston all appreciate and revere you. It would be wrong . . . in fact almost . . . wicked that somebody as unimportant as myself should damage the . . . respect in which you are held."

"And you really think my association with you would do that?" Lord Charnock asked.

It sounds as if I am being . . . conceited to . . . think so," Zelina said humbly, "but I heard the things the ladies who visited the Princess said about you, and I am sure they are no different from Aunt Kathleen's friends. They would talk and . . . talk, and there would be nothing you could do about it."

"So to save me from a lot of chattering women," Lord Charnock answered, "you are prepared to risk being as frightened as you were when I heard you scream in the Writing-Room of the ship, and again when you were clever enough last night to hide from Prince Alexis."

"I . . . I am thinking of you . . . only of you."

"I am deeply touched by your concern, but I still want to know why," Lord Charnock persisted.

Zelina knew there was a very easy answer, but it was one she could not give him.

She could only look away and murmur again:

"You have been . . . so kind . . . to me."

"That is not exactly what I wanted to hear," Lord Charnock said, "but now let me tell you my suggestion. You have told me what you suggest you should do. Now please listen to me."

It flashed through Zelina's mind that he was going to suggest that he should leave her in Copenhagen with Sir Henry Watkin Williams-Winn or perhaps with the British Minister in Kiev.

There at least she might find somebody to travel with her on the journey home and that would be better than travelling alone.

"What I have been thinking," Lord Charnock was saying quietly, "is that even if you come with me on the ship that is waiting in the harbour, we will still leave behind a lot of speculation amongst the Russians. As you have so rightly discovered, women of every nation are compulsive talkers and they will undoubtedly find a very obvious reason for your precipitate departure from Tsarskoye Selo."

Zelina clasped her fingers together so tightly that the nails dug into her skin.

Then she said in a voice that was barely audible:

"It was . . . wrong of me to . . . force myself on you. I will go back and . . . apologise."

"Do you really think I would let you do such a thing?" He spoke almost roughly, and, startled, she raised her eyes to his.

He was looking at her in a way that held her spellbound, and he said:

"You have not yet heard my suggestion."

"W-what . . . is it?"

It was difficult for her to speak.

"The only reasonable explanation for your joining me after I had said good-bye to the Tsar, and the only way we can travel together without there being any scandal, is that you should marry me!"

For a moment Zelina thought she could not have heard the last words but only imagined them.

"M-marry . . . you?"

"I have in fact already arranged it," Lord Charnock said, "and the Chaplain is waiting for us in the Embassy Church which adjoins this house."

Zelina felt as if she had stepped into a dream and that neither she nor Lord Charnock had any reality but were figments of her imagination.

"What are you . . . saying? . . . You cannot mean . . . !" she stammered.

"I mean that I want to look after you, Zelina. To protect you and keep you safe from ever being afraid of anything as you are now, and the only way I can do that is for you to become my wife."

"B-but . . . you do not really . . . want me."

He smiled, and Zelina felt as if the room were suddenly lit with a thousand candles.

"I will tell you how much I want you," he said, "but after we are married. Now the ship is waiting."

Zelina drew in her breath.

Then, as if she felt that she must hold on to him to make sure that what he was saying was real and she was not in fact asleep, she put out her hands and he took them in his.

He raised first one, then the other to his lips and she felt a thrill go through her. Then as he lifted his head to look at her again, the door opened and the Earl of Durham came into the Salon.

"I heard you were back," he said to Lord Charnock. "Miss Tiverton, it is delightful to see you again!"

With an effort Zelina remembered to curtsey, and the Earl went on:

"Everything is arranged. My Chaplain is waiting, and I hope, Miss Tiverton, you will permit me to give you away."

"Th-thank you," Zelina stammered.

"It will be correct, Charnock, for you to go ahead of us," the Earl said, "and the First Secretary is waiting in the Hall, who will, he assures me, be delighted to act as your Best Man."

"I appreciate your efficiency, Your Excellency."

Lord Charnock smiled at Zelina again and the look in his eyes made her feel as if he were touching her.

Then he went from the Salon, and she wanted to run after him to make sure that he would not change his mind and he had really in fact said they were to be married.

The Earl held out his arm.

"Your prospective husband is waiting," he said. "He has taken us by surprise, but I hope that because we are all British here, we can cope with any emergency, even a wedding which is taking place in an unprecedented hurry."

He did not seem to expect an answer, and Zelina was incapable of giving one.

It was impossible to think of anything the Earl was saying in his pompous voice, because her heart was throbbing in a manner which made it difficult to breathe and she felt as if the whole world had turned topsy-turvey and would never right itself again.

It could not be true that she was to be married to a man to whom she had already given her heart, when she had never suspected that he thought of her in any way except as a rather tiresome, bothersome child.

'I love him!' she thought as they proceeded down the long corridor. 'I love him so much . . . so please . . . God, make him love me.'

The Embassy Church was small but beautifully constructed, and the Altar was decorated with flowers.

Even when Zelina saw the Chaplain waiting in his white surplice she still could not believe she was actually being married. Yet, Lord Charnock was standing there, and as if he knew what she was feeling he put out his hand and took hers.

The Parson read the opening words of the Service, the British Ambassador gave Zelina away, and the First Secretary produced a ring which Lord Charnock put on her finger.

It was only when it was actually on that she realised it was the signet-ring that he wore on the smallest finger of his left hand, but even so it was too large for her.

It symbolised all she longed for and all she had ever imagined in her wildest dreams would ever come true.

She was married to a man who stood for safety and security and whom she loved with her heart and soul.

Lord Charnock said his vows in a deep voice with unmistakable sincerity, and the Parson blessed them.

As Zelina took his arm for him to lead her from the small Chapel, she was still praying that as her husband Lord Charnock might love her even a small fraction as much as she loved him.

They walked back into the small Drawing-Room where they had been before, and now there was champagne waiting for them.

The Earl raised his glass.

"May you have many years of great happiness!" he said.

"Thank you," Lord Charnock replied. "We shall always be extremely grateful to Your Excellency for facilitating our wedding."

"It was certainly a surprise," the Earl replied, "but I think we rose to the emergency in the way you would expect."

Lord Charnock turned to Zelina and raised his glass.

"To my bride!" he said softly, and she blushed.

"I am going to suggest that while your luggage is taken aboard, you have a light luncheon," the Earl said. "I have also instructed my servants to inform the Captain that you will be ready to leave on the afternoon tide."

"That is what I wish," Lord Charnock agreed.

* * *

Afterwards, Zelina could never remember what she ate or what had been said at the luncheon in the impressive Dining-Room where she had dined with a large party three days after she had arrived at the Volkonsky Palace.

Now just the four of them sat at the small table in the window, and she had never known Lord Charnock to be in such good spirits and so witty and amusing.

Even the Earl forgot to be pompous and tried to cap Lord Charnock's stories, while the First Secretary could only laugh helplessly and seemed to enjoy himself as if he were a boy being given an unexpected treat by his Seniors.

To Zelina it was all unreal, and yet it was so exciting that she felt as if she were a spectator in a Theatre and that a drama was unfolding itself in front of her eyes.

When the luncheon was finished she went upstairs to put on her bonnet, which she had removed before they ate, then she came down carrying a travelling-cloak to put over her gown, and found Lord Charnock waiting for her in the Hall.

Because he was watching her descending the stairs, she suddenly felt shy and found it impossible to meet his eyes.

She was going away with him to start a new life, and for the moment she could not speculate what this would be. She knew only that because she was with him it would be like starting on a journey to Paradise.

She had almost reached the foot of the stairs when there was the sound of voices at the front door, and as she saw Lord Charnock and the Ambassador turn their heads, Prince Alexis came past the servants to stand in front of them.

He was wearing riding-clothes and Zelina had the impression from the dust on his boots and his general appearance that he had ridden fast and furiously.

Walking straight up to Lord Charnock and facing him, he said in a voice of anger that seemed to ring out:

"How dare you abduct one of the Tsar's guests! His Imperial Majesty has deputed me to bring back Miss Tiverton immediately to the Prince and Princess Volkonsky, to whom her aunt entrusted her!"

The Prince seemed almost to shout the last words at Lord Charnock, and Zelina felt with a sudden constriction of her heart that it would be impossible for his request to be refused.

Then even before Lord Charnock spoke she knew that her fears were quite unnecessary.

He looked at the Prince in a manner which any other man would have found extremely intimidating.

"I must regret, Your Highness," he said slowly, "that your journey to St. Petersburg is a waste of time. You should have stayed in the country and enjoyed the spoils of the chase."

There was no doubt that Lord Charnock meant to

be offensive, and there was an innuendo behind his words.

The Prince, however, retorted furiously:

"You may try to bluster your way out of this, Charnock, but while you are in this country you will obey the laws of the land, and the Tsar insists on Miss Tiverton's return."

"At your instigation, I presume!" Lord Charnock said.

"I do not have to answer your questions," the Prince retorted.

He turned to the Earl to say:

"As British Ambassador, Your Excellency is aware that Miss Tiverton may be hiding here on what you consider British soil, but if she sets one foot outside the Embassy she can be arrested for not complying with what is an Imperial Order!"

The Earl was taller than the Prince, and he drew himself up to his full height and replied in his usual pompous manner, which was somehow more effective than anything the Prince had said because it was calm and clear:

"I am, Your Highness, fully familiar with both the laws of Russia and the privilege accorded to Diplomats. You are informing me, I understand, that His Imperial Majesty requires the return to Tsarskoye Selo of Miss Zelina Tiverton under escort by Your Highness."

"Exactly!" the Prince snapped. "And now inform Miss Tiverton that I am here and a carriage should be arriving for her at any moment."

"You have your instructions in writing, I presume?" the Earl asked.

"Then you presume wrong!" the Prince replied. "At the same time, I cannot believe that you are questioning my word as a gentleman and an Officer of the Imperial Guard."

"No, Your Highness, I would not think of doing such a thing!" the Earl replied. "But your request is for Miss Zelina Tiverton."

"Good God!" the Prince ejaculated in an exasperated tone. "I do not have to repeat it, do I? She was carried here in Charnock's carriages after he persuaded her to behave in this outrageous manner. But I will see that she does not suffer from his rudeness, which is an insult to her host and hostess."

"That is very generous of you," Lord Charnock said sarcastically.

Zelina could see that he was growing angrier with the Prince, and she was wondering whether she should intervene, when the Earl said:

"I must ask Your Highness to convey to His Imperial Majesty my most sincere apologies for the impetuous manner in which Miss Tiverton left Tsarskoye Selo, but I know her excuse is one which will be readily accepted both by His Imperial Majesty and by the warm-hearted Tsarina . . ."

"Miss Tiverton can make her own apologies," the Prince interrupted. "Do as I have already asked, and inform her that I am here!"

"That is something I am unfortunately unable to do," the Earl replied.

"Why? Where has she gone?" the Prince shouted.

"Miss Zelina Tiverton no longer exists," the Ambassador said quietly. "She is in fact now Lady Charnock, and I know Your Highness will wish to be the first to congratulate His Lordship and wish them both every happiness."

As the Ambassador spoke he looked towards Zelina where she was standing on the last step of the stairway, holding on to the bannisters, her eyes wide and frightened in her pale face.

Suddenly aware of her presence, the Prince swung round on his heel to face her.

Then for a moment he was still, before he asked in a voice that was very different from the one in which he had been shouting angrily at the Ambassador:

"You are married?"

"Y-yes . . ."

Because she was frightened she wanted to run to Lord Charnock, but she was unable to move and could only stand where she was, holding on to the bannisters as if they would prevent her from falling.

Then Lord Charnock was beside her, holding out his arm.

"Come," he said quietly. "We must leave for the ship or we may miss the tide."

As she put her arm into his, Zelina was suddenly aware that her fear had left her.

It was not only because of the expression of frustration on the Prince's face, but because Lord Charnock gave her a feeling of security that was unlike anything she had ever known before.

She murmured her farewells to the Earl as they walked down the steps, and as they got into the carriage she was thinking only that she was safe.

Safe from the Prince, from Russia, from men like Adamson, safe from anything and everything that might frighten her in the future, and safe from being alone and helpless.

They drove away and Zelina had the impression, although she could not be certain, that the Prince had not moved, but still stood where they had left him, unable to readjust himself to a situation in which he had been vanquished and there was nothing he could do about it.

It was only when they were some way from the Embassy that Lord Charnock said:

"I am sorry that had to happen, but I know you will be sensible enough to forget it and not let it spoil our wedding-day."

"I am . . . really married to . . . you?" Zelina asked in a small voice.

"I promise you it is absolutely legal according to English Law, and I think we both felt that we received the blessing of the Church."

"The Service was very . . . beautiful and just the way I would have . . . wished to be . . . married."

"You surprise me!" Lord Charnock answered. "I thought that every woman wanted bride's-maids, a huge congregation of friends, and a Reception afterwards."

Zelina laughed.

"That is something I would have hated! The only person I . . . really wanted at my . . . wedding was . . . you!"

"That is something I should have said first," Lord Charnock smiled, "but we have not had much time for conversation, which is something we can make up for in the ship."

As he spoke he took her hand in his and, gently pulling off her travelling-glove, raised it to his lips.

"Now that I have seen what the Prince can be like," he said quietly, "I realise how brave you have been!"

"I think the only . . . brave thing I did . . . was to run . . . away to . . . you."

Lord Charnock kissed her hand again. Then, because words were unnecessary, she held on to him tightly until they reached the harbour.

H.M.S. Dolphin, the British flag, looked extremely impressive, and when they were piped aboard the Captain was waiting to receive them.

"Welcome, My Lord," he said to Lord Charnock, "and very sincere congratulations on behalf of myself and my crew."

"Thank you," Lord Charnock replied.

He presented the Captain to Zelina, after which the Captain presented his officers before he said:

"I have put my own cabins at your disposal, My Lord. And now, if you will excuse me, we have to move out to sea with all possible speed, otherwise we shall be in danger of running aground on a sand-bank."

"That is certainly something which must not happen," Lord Charnock remarked.

The Captain left them and another officer escorted them below-decks to where the two cabins which had been allotted to them seemed to Zelina very palatial.

They were not so luxuriously decorated as the *Ischora*, but the Sitting-Cabin was comfortably furnished and had a long table at which the Captain could entertain when he wished to do so.

In the Sleeping-Cabin there was a large curtained four-poster which made Zelina blush when she looked at it.

Her trunks were already neatly arranged so as not to be obstructive, and a man was already unpacking one of them for her.

She looked in surprise at Lord Charnock, who explained:

"This is Hibbert, my valet, and I assure you he will prove an extremely efficient lady's-maid until I can engage one for you, which will not be until we reach England."

"I'll do my best to look after you, M'Lady," Hibbert said with a grin.

Zelina smiled back at him a little shyly, finding it strange to be addressed by her new title.

Then she and Lord Charnock went back into the Saloon and they were alone.

She looked at him a little uncertainly, feeling shy and yet excited. But there was still that dream-like quality about everything which she had felt ever since she had reached the British Embassy.

"You are safe now," Lord Charnock said. "You are on a British ship and in a few minutes we shall be leaving Russia for what I hope will be a very long time."

"I hope so . . . too," Zelina said, "but . . . how can I . . . thank you?"

"I can think of a lot of answers to that question," Lord Charnock replied, "but first I suggest you take off your cloak and bonnet."

Zelina raised her hands to do so, but he was beside her and undid the ribbons of her bonnet, lifting it from her head.

He threw it down on a chair, then unclasped the light cloak she wore over her gown and threw that after it.

He stood looking at her and she felt a sudden awareness of him in a way that was so exciting that it was difficult to breathe.

"You are very beautiful, Zelina!" he said after a moment.

"Do you . . . really think so?" she asked. "When I saw the . . . beautiful Russian ladies, I was so afraid that you would . . . think it impossible to . . . find me even . . . pretty."

He knew she was thinking of the Countess Natasha, and he smiled as he said:

"I thought you very lovely the first time I saw you. Then your face began to haunt me, and it was difficult to look at any other woman without seeing you."

"Is that . . . true?" Zelina asked.

"I tried not to believe it," Lord Charnock said, "just as I tried not to become too involved with you, my darling."

"I . . . I tried not to . . . bother you."

"Perhaps neither of us tried hard enough," he said, "or perhaps Fate was stronger than all our efforts to escape from each other."

"I did not . . . wish to escape . . . . I was only afraid that you would . . . leave me."

"That was what I meant to do," he said. "Then

when you put your hand into mine in the carriage, I knew that I loved you as I have never loved a woman before."

He made an exasperated sound as he said:

"It is something I have been feeling ever since you asked me to help you, but I was so certain that I would never love anybody enough to marry them that I told myself you could mean nothing in my life and I must keep you out of it."

"But you . . . really did . . . want to . . . marry me?"

"I promised myself I would tell you how much," Lord Charnock replied, "but it is something which is difficult to put into words."

He put his arms round her as he spoke and pulled her against him.

She lifted her face and he looked down at her for a long moment before his lips found hers.

As he kissed her Zelina knew that this was what she had been wanting and longing for ever since they had been together on the *Ischora*.

It was then, she thought, that she had fallen in love with him. It had been impossible to think of anything but him, and he had been in her thoughts from first thing in the morning to last thing at night.

Lord Charnock's lips were gentle and tender, and as he felt her mouth quiver beneath his he knew it was the first time she had been kissed, and how innocent and inexperienced she was.

Then the rapture and excitement rising in Zelina aroused the same feeling in him, so that he knew this kiss was very different from anything he had ever given to or received from a woman before.

To Zelina it was a kiss that had a wonder and a glory which was part of Heaven itself, and at the same time it had the thrill and excitement that she had felt as she had watched the gypsy dancers and heard them sing.

It all seemed to mingle into an inexpressible rapture and was so amazing that she could not think clearly, but could only feel as if her whole body vibrated to a music that was part of the Divine and yet somehow at the same time was very human.

Only when she felt as if she were floating in the sky and her feet were no longer on the ground did Lord Charnock raise his head, and she said a little incoherently:

"I . . . love you! I . . . love . . . you! Please . . . love me a little . . . too."

Do you think this is a little?" Lord Charnock asked.

Then he was kissing her again, demandingly, fiercely, insistently, as if he wooed her with his lips and she must surrender herself completely.

*   *   *

Later, as the ship gathered speed, Lord Charnock drew Zelina to a sofa and they sat down, his arms round her, her head on his shoulder.

"How can you make me feel like this?" he asked in his deep voice. "I was sure that all I had to do, my darling one, was to teach you about love, but now I realise that I too have a lot to learn."

"I . . . want to make you . . . happy."

"I am happy," he answered, "so happy that I am no longer myself but somebody so strange that I almost feel I need to be introduced to him!"

Zelina laughed.

"How exciting it will be to get to . . . know you . . . but I love and . . . adore what I . . . already know."

"My precious," Lord Charnock said, "when you say things like that, I realise how incredibly lucky I am to have found you."

"No, I am the lucky one," Zelina said, "I used to imagine what the man I would marry would be like, but

I could never have imagined anybody as wonderful or as marvellous as you!"

She moved a little nearer to him as she said:

"I did not . . . want to come to Russia. I . . . hated the . . . idea of it. But how could I know that in . . . doing so I would find . . . you?"

"I thought the same," Lord Charnock agreed. "I had no wish to leave London."

As he spoke, he remembered that one of his reasons for wishing to refuse Lord Palmerston's request was a very attractive woman in whom he had been interested.

Now she seemed only a pale ghost and it was hard to remember even what she looked like.

As if Zelina knew what he was thinking, she said:

"When you know me . . . better, you may find me . . . disappointing . . . after all the lovely ladies you have . . . loved in the . . . past."

"I have never loved anybody as I love you," Lord Charnock said, "and I know that I shall not be disappointed, my precious."

"How can you be . . . certain?"

"Because I have never before been in love with anybody who was so young and so innocent was prepared for me to teach her."

His arms tightened round Zelina as he asked:

"You are willing for me to do that?"

"You know I . . . want you to . . . teach me," Zelina replied, "and I cannot imagine anything more . . . utterly glorious or perfect than that you . . . should teach me about . . . love."

She hid her face against him as she added:

"I am afraid I am . . . very . . . very ignorant about it . . . except that I know what I . . . feel for you is the love which comes from God."

"Our lessons, my adorable one, will be not only thrilling but something that will last us for the rest of our lives. We have so much to discover about each other, so much to do in the future, and I know that just as you need me, I need you."

"You are . . . sure of . . . that?"

"Very sure. You have already helped me," Lord Charnock replied. "Do you realise, my clever little wife, that the information you gave me by listening to Count Nesselrode and Baron Brunnow was what I came to Russia to discover? But for you I should have had to admit that I had failed."

Zelina drew in her breath with excitement.

"Is that . . . really true? Have I . . . really been of help?"

"A very great help indeed! And if I had not loved you and married you I would still have been obliged to take you away from Russia, just in case by sheer deduction the Prince discovered how you had been able to hide from him."

"But you did marry me!"

"Yes, my darling, and I swear I will never allow you to regret it."

"As though I would!" Zelina cried. "I am going to thank God every day of my life, as I thanked Him today in the Church, that you should want me and love me."

"I love you with my heart and my soul—if I have one—and my body," Lord Charnock said.

He put his fingers under her chin and turned her face up to his as he spoke.

Then he was kissing her again, kissing her more passionately, more insistently than he had done before, and Zelina could feel his heart beating against her breast and knew that she excited him.

*   *   *

Very much later, when *H.M.S. Dolphin* was moving over the open sea and the Captain was looking for a sheltered place in which to anchor during the night, Zelina stirred against Lord Charnock's shoulder.

In the big four-poster bed which Hibbert had made up with Lord Charnock's own sheets, with which he always travelled, she felt that she was in a small, enchanted ship of their own.

A ship within a ship, in which, as she had once wanted to do, they could sail away to a magical horizon, never to return.

"Do you . . . still love me?" she whispered, and felt Lord Charnock hold her closer against him.

"That is something I should be asking you, my darling," he said. "You are quite certain I have not frightened you?"

"You could never frighten me," Zelina said. "When I am close to you, I am safe, and I know that . . . nothing can . . . hurt me."

He kissed her forehead and she whispered:

"It was so wonderful when you . . . loved me . . . it was like watching the gypsies dance and hearing their music, and yet what was happening was all part of the stars."

"My precious, that is what I wanted you to feel."

"Was it . . . wonderful for you . . . too?"

He heard the anxiety in her voice and knew it was something she had been wanting to ask him.

"Like you," he said in his deep voice, "I had no idea love could be so perfect, so beautiful. That is what you have brought me, Zelina—beauty! A beauty I swear to you I have never known before in my whole life."

She gave a little cry and reached up her arms to pull his head down to hers.

"You . . . swear to me that is . . . true?"

"I swear it! And it is something I shall want to go on proving to you over and over again, my beautiful little wife."

"I . . . adore you . . . I . . . worship you," Zelina said softly.

Then, as if he had no words in which to reply, Lord Charnock was kissing her and once again there was the wild, ecstatic music of the gypsy violins.

The stars fell down from the sky to make them one, and there was no more fear—only love.

ABOUT THE AUTHOR

BARBARA CARTLAND, the world's most famous romantic novelist, who is also an historian, playwright, lecturer, political speaker and television personality, has now written over 300 books.

She has also had many historical works published and has written four autobiographies as well as the biographies of her mother and that of her brother Ronald Cartland, who was the first Member of Parliament to be killed in W.W. II. This book has a preface by Sir Winston Churchill and has just been republished with an introduction by Sir Arthur Bryant.

Barbara Cartland has sold 200 million books over the world, more than half of these in the U.S.A. She broke the world record in 1975 by writing twenty-three books and the four subsequent years with 20, 21, 23 and 24. In addition her album of love songs has just been published, sung with the Royal Philharmonic Orchestra.

Barbara Cartland, who is a Dame of the Order of St. John of Jerusalem has championed the cause for old people and founded the first Romany Gypsy Camp in the world.

Barbara Cartland is deeply interested in Vitamin Therapy and is President of the British National Association for Health. Her book the *Magic of Honey* has sold in millions all over the world.

She has a magazine *The World of Romance* and her Barbara Cartland Romantic World Tours will, in conjunction with British Airways, carry travelers to England, Egypt, India, France, Germany and Turkey.

Barbara Cartland

The world's bestselling author of romantic fiction. Her stories are always captivating tales of intrigue, adventure and love.

☐	13830	THE DAWN OF LOVE	$1.75
☐	14791	NIGHT OF GAIETY	$1.95
☐	14503	THE LIONESS AND THE LILY	$1.75
☐	13942	LUCIFER AND THE ANGEL	$1.75
☐	14084	OLA AND THE SEA WOLF	$1.75
☐	14133	THE PRUDE AND THE PRODIGAL	$1.75
☐	13032	PRIDE AND THE POOR PRINCESS	$1.75
☐	13984	LOVE FOR SALE	$1.75
☐	14248	THE GODDESS AND THE GAIETY GIRL	$1.75
☐	14360	SIGNPOST TO LOVE	$1.75
☐	14361	FROM HELL TO HEAVEN	$1.75
☐	14585	LOVE IN THE MOON	$1.95
☐	13985	LOST LAUGHTER	$1.75
☐	14750	DREAMS DO COME TRUE	$1.95
☐	14902	WINGED MAGIC	$1.95
☐	14922	A PORTRAIT OF LOVE	$1.95

Buy them at your local bookstore or use this handy coupon: